Other Books
By
Robert J. McHatton

THE DIRTY DEED
MY KIDS
BONUS TIME AND OTHER STORIES

Films
By
Robert J. McHatton

THE RED SUIT
ARREST MOMMY
DUCT TAPE
UMATILLA
SHIP OF MIRACLES

The Brilliants

Three Novellas

Robert J. McHatton

Order this book online at www.trafford.com
or email orders@trafford.com

Most Trafford titles are also available at
major online book retailers.

This is a work of fiction. Any resemblance to a
real person or events is purely coincidental.

Visit the author's websites at

www.whiteknuckles.com
www.rjmchatton.com
www.inventiveproductions.com

Printed in the United States of America.

ISBN: 978-1-4251-1287-5 (sc)

Trafford rev. 07/29/2013

www.trafford.com

North America & international
toll-free: 1 888 232 4444 (USA & Canada)
fax: 812 355 4082

DEDICATION:

To my Mom, who always believed in me.

Contents

"The Brilliants"

A bland grayness filled the air. Short breathing sounds, then a clapping noise could be heard in the distance.

It was a smoky foggy day. The clouds moved quickly and abundantly, allowing a maze of shadows to take control.

Puffs of smoke rose through the fog, until finally the face of a big horse appeared. It coughed.

The hoofs clapped along the wet black street. The horse's head bobbed up and down. The horse pulled a long cart. The cart was carrying a large wooden box.

The cart slowly made its way up the brick road. Three people walked behind the cart on its way to the gravesite.

A preacher held tightly to an open bible as he looked over an open grave.

"And, Lord, may you have mercy on this humble man, for he was only a single servant, but a creative and loving one, Lord."

As the preacher continued his prayer, the fog began to lift to show the faces in the crowd. One was J.T. Smith, an aged man and the other, Henry, a scrawny gravedigger. Henry did not seem too emotional that day. His teethed clawed down on chewing tobacco.

The preacher said, "May he rest in peace. In the name of the Father, Son, and Holy Spirit."

JT said, "Amen."

Henry threw a pile of dirt onto the box.

JT walked slowly through the crowded streets. The

walkways of London were very full that day in 1827.

JT seemed emotionless as he continued his journey. Along the way he stopped at a street vendor to buy a newspaper.

JT headed towards a boarding house. A couple of old ladies stood out front.

"Good morning, Mister Smith."

JT did nothing to show he even heard her.

The other woman said, "It's a right beautiful day, Mister Smith."

Without saying a word, JT entered the building.

"Well, I never!" said the woman.

JT entered the apartment, taking off his coat. Several paintings were on easels, in frames, and every which way throughout the room.

JT walked over to a half-finished painting. He shook his head.

He picked up the newspaper. The title said, "Gentleman's Magazine."

He fished through the pages until he stopped at one with the headline "Obituaries."

JT was very angry. He walked over to the half-empty easel. Then he knocked it to the ground.

Suddenly he realized what he had done. He quickly picked up the easel, handling it with care.

"Sorry," he said to the easel.

He looked around the apartment. Then he went to the kitchen and poured himself a drink.

JT slammed the drink down his throat. Then he picked up a feather pen. He dipped it into an inkwell.

Slowly he began to write:

"A letter to the editor"

He poured himself another drink.

"Here is an obituary you forgot to include in your publication."

JT looked deep in thought. He looked over to the half-empty easel.

The feather pen continued, "Mister Thomas Rowlandson was my friend."

JT downed a shot of whiskey. He started singing, "Lo, what splendors round us darling. Swift illume the charming scene . . ."

Back to the paper, he wrote "I first met him in a place called Vauxhall Gardens."

He looked over to a painting on the wall of a wonderful garden.

The roulette wheel spun endlessly, it seemed, until finally the little ball dropped.

A crowd of people suddenly burst into a loud cheer and applause.

The room was smoky and full of loud music.

A man played a violin. People stood around another man on a soapbox.

The room was very busy that day. Dance hall girls

were dancing, bartenders were mixing, and people were laughing.

In the corner, a large group of people stood around what appeared to be a poker game.

This was a poker game of all poker games. Several men were playing.

One man was a slender, good looking gent, his name was John Bannister. Another one was a short and stocky fellow named Angelo. One man wore a proper dark business man suit. He was Matthew. And in the corner of the room, was a tall, strikingly handsome Thomas Rowlandson.

Bannister held his hand close. "Gentlemen, what is the bet?"

"Five," said Angelo.

Bannister moved his eyes back and forth.

"Five, eh," he said. Then he smiled, "I see no problems for me. I will raise you five more."

Matthew, the businessman, quipped, "Well my friends,

since this is a friendly game."

They all laughed.

"It took me forty years to learn the value of money, so I think I will put this knowledge to good use."

He laid his cards down on the table, folding.

Rowlandson said, "Well, gentlemen, I can truly say that I am lucky that I can call you my friends."

They looked at their cards.

Rowlandson continued, "But, friends, I must do something I truly dread."

He downed a drink.

Angelo yelled, "Rolly, we do not need speeches."

Rowlandson replied, "Very well, Angelo, I will see yours, and raise you forty."

Rowlandson swished his drink with his finger. There was quite a stir in the crowd.

Angelo said, "Forty? Rolly, what are you doing?"

Rowlandson said, "Do not worry yourself so, Angelo. You are a wealthy man and can afford it. Me, I am not wealthy. Well, I am wealthy, but my wealth lies in the fingers of my hands."

Bannister said, "You painters are so flamboyant. Look at me. All I have to sell is my performance as an actor."

A horse drawn buggy rode up to the casino. Out came a young man, JT Smith. He was accompanied by a delicate beauty, Betty.

JT said, "Vauxhall Gardens. Betty, this is where the best dressed, well mannered people go."

He helped her from the carriage. Their eyes locked in sync. They were in love.

Betty's eyes had a softness to them.

She said, "Jay, I am so happy."

They hugged.

"Jay?" she asked.

"Yes, my darling?" He could not keep his eyes off her.

She whispered, "I love you."

He smiled, "you are so precious."

Inside the casino, a group of musicians began to play.

JT and Betty entered, sort of pushing their way through a crowd.

Rowlandson looked up to see JT and Betty. He looked close on Betty. She looked so young and innocent as they were seated to a table.

Angelo threw his cards into a pile on the table.

He said, "Dammit, Rolly, I cannot believe your luck."

Rowlandson smiled as he pulled in the pot of money.

"It's not luck, Angelo," he said. "To call this luck is the same as my calling your expertise as a swordsman luck. This isn't luck."

Bannister said, "No, I call it nerve."

Rowlandson laughed. He lit a big cigar, looked over to Betty, and then back to the table.

He said, "Nerve is in the eye of the beholder.

Gentlemen, I just live by one credo. See what you want and get it."

Angelo noticed Rowlandson's leers at Betty.

He said, "And you are not just talking about card games."

"No," said Rowlandson. "Does anyone have any knowledge about that young man and his friend?"

Bannister said, "Oh, that's that young draftsman son of Allison Smith."

Angelo pointed at Rowlandson, "We should feel thankful to see a great womanizer's mind at work."

Rowlandson shook his head, "and his name?"

Bannister said, "John. John T. Smith. But Rolly, he is a nice young man, with ideals and ambitions. Remember when you were idealistic, so long ago?"

Rowlandson said, "Don't worry. I am just curious."

Angelo said, "Curiosity of the wolf."

They laughed. Rowlandson got up out of his chair, downed his drink, and put out his cigar.

JT and Betty sipped their wine, listening to the music.

JT said, "This seems to be a nice place."

Betty noticed Rowlandson approaching.

"Yes, it does," she said.

JT asked, "are you having a good time?"

Betty smiled, "anytime I am with you."

Rowlandson came up to their table.

"Excuse me," he said.

"Yes?" said JT.

Rowlandson said, "please excuse me for intruding, but my friend over there . . . ."

He pointed over to the group of poker players. They were watching intently.

Rowlandson continued, "My friend Mister John Bannister has told me that you are a colleague of mine."

JT said, "a colleague?"

"Yes," he said. "He tells me that you are a draftsman and well, let me introduce myself. My name is Thomas Rowlandson."

JT and Betty were surprised.

Betty asked, "the painter?"

Rowlandson replied, "Yes, I dabble into a painting here and there."

JT stood up, "Mister Rowlandson, I am humbled that you should call me a colleague."

Rowlandson smiled, "Nonsense. I consider my paintings to be drafting of a sense."

JT seemed in awe. He quickly asked, "Please, let me buy you a drink."

Rowlandson said, "No, that is not necessary."

Betty said, "Please, Mister Rowlandson, it is our pleasure."

Rowlandson smiled, "Well, if you insist."

The band played a fun song. A big chested woman began

to sing and the entire room joined in.

Hours later, JT laughed hysterically with Rowlandson and Betty.

JT said, "That was a fantastic story." He was almost drunk.

He continued, "Gosh, Mister Rowlandson, I cannot believe that I am actually talking to the painter of the great painting Gardens of Vauxhall, and we are right this moment in the actual location where it was drawn."

Looking over at Betty, Rowlandson said, "Call me Rolly, Jay, my friends do."

JT said, "Thank you, Rolly."

Rowlandson told Betty, "Please, Miss Winter, uh, Betty, call me Rolly."

Betty replied, "thank you, Mister Rowlandson."

Rowlandson stood up, "Well I have to be going now. My friends seem to need my guidance."

The poker gang laughed.

Rowlandson gently grabbed Betty's hand, "I am very pleased to have met you, Miss Winter."

Then he turned to JT and shook his hand, "and you, Mister Smith."

JT said, "The pleasure has been ours."

Rowlandson swung his arms as he spoke, "I have an idea, Jay. I am going to the country tomorrow to work on a drawing. Won't you and Miss Winter join me?"

Betty said, "I don't know."

JT grinned, "That is very nice of you, Rolly.

Rowlandson said, "Well then it is settled." He kissed Betty's hand and exited.

JT said, "Wait till my father hears that we spent the evening with a famous painter, an artist. And yet, he is such a nice fellow."

Betty grabbed his arm, "Let's be gone, Jay."

She pulled at him and led him out.

A carriage sped down a trail in the beautiful English countryside.

Rowlandson, JT, and Betty were sitting happily, watching as the landscape passed by.

The green rolling hills were breathtaking that day.

After they stopped the carriage, Betty looked out at the incredible scenery. She turned and ran down the hill to the picnic area, where Rowlandson stood in front of an easel. Behind him was JT, watching Rolly's every move in awe. JT held his head, still hurting from his hangover.

Betty said, "It is so beautiful here."

Rowlandson looked over to JT. "I have found the best remedy for headaches in the morning. It is taking a pen or brush into my hand in the cool breeze of the country, the company of a beautiful young woman, and a big swig from this container of a very special home remedy."

He handed JT a small brown flask. JT swallowed the liquid and flinched from its strength.

Rowlandson laughed, "I never said it tasted good. Only that it takes the pain away."

In the distance, they could hear a big bird chirping.

Betty remarked, "what a cute bird."

Rowlandson said, "That is Harry. An old friend of mine."

JT asked, "Harry the bird?"

Rowlandson nodded, "we go way back to when I first started drawing."

JT looked up at the bird.

Rowlandson continued, "Harry's singing has inspired many an easel."

Betty asked, "what makes you paint? Have you always done it?"

Rowlandson drank some of the liquid from the boga bag.

"Miss Winter, I was blessed early on with a flair for drawing."

He drank another swig.

"Thanks to a wealthy aunt who sent me to the best art school in Paris."

JT said, "the Royal Academy?"

"Yes," exclaimed Rolly. "My dear old aunt helped me then and bless her soul she helps me now."

Betty said, "She sounds like a very nice woman."

Rowlandson said, "May she rest in peace."

JT and Betty looked at each other as Rolly downed more liquid.

"Don't worry," Rolly said. "My aunt was a good woman who supported my career for a long time, and thanks to her will, she supports me now.

He took a big swig and laughed.

Betty asked, "What are you painting?"

Looking closely at the painting, it appeared to be a city street full of people.

Rowlandson said, "It is just an early sketch."

JT said, "I would have thought you would have to be in the city to draw it."

Betty exclaimed, "Incredible."

Rowlandson said, "I paint and sketch visions. What I see. But enough for today. Let's go. I have an appointment with a very important gentleman and you are invited."

He got up and started packing his easel. JT looked over at Betty.

The Prince of Wales stood frozen.

"How long must I stand here? It seems like I have been here for days. Aren't you done yet?"

Rowlandson sketched continuously. Betty, JT, and several other people watched his every move.

Rowlandson said, "It takes time for perfection, Prince."

The Prince tried not to move when he replied, "I know, I know. Just do it right, Rowlandson."

Rolly said, "You will not be sorry, Prince. My clients never are sorry."

JT whispered to Betty, "Betty, that man is the Prince of Wales. Can you believe we are actually here watching his portrait being painted?

Betty said, "SSHHH, Jay."

JT said, "Just imagine, this painting could be placed in the Queen's palace."

Betty could not take her eyes off Rowlandson.

She said, "I am beginning to believe what they say about this man, Thomas Rowlandson."

Rowlandson said, "Alright, Prince, you can take a break. I am done for today."

He packed up his easel.

The Prince replied, "Well, it's about time. I have never seen anyone work like this."

Rowlandson became angry, "Prince, I work my own way. I always have. You hired me to paint your portrait. I assumed you wanted it done right. If you don't, tell me. I won't mind at all."

The Prince shouted, "I am shocked."

Rowlandson responded, "Well? Should I return tomorrow?"

The Prince was silent for a moment. Then he said, "Mister Rowlandson, I do not like your attitude or your style, but I do like your paintings, so please let us finish soon and I will forget what you just said."

Rowlandson said, "I will be done soon, and you will not be disappointed."

The crowd waited. The easel was covered by a velvet drapery.

The audience started getting antsy.

The drapery was pulled back to reveal a great portrait of the Prince of Wales.

The audience applauded and cheered. The Prince and Rowlandson stood alone.

The Prince shouted, "Oh, my God, it is beautiful."

He looked to Rolly.

"Mister Rowlandson," he said. "I love it. I actually love it. Please how can I possibly thank you?"

Rowlandson said, "No thanks are necessary, Prince. The portrait speaks for itself."

The Prince laughed, "and the subject."

The crowd laughed, but Rowlandson didn't. He went through the crowd to JT and Betty who are in the back.

Rowlandson said, "Ready for a party. What are we waiting for?"

Betty and JT smiled roarously.

Inside the cabaret, a beautiful woman sang a Johann Christian Bach song. There were organists and violinists playing in unison.

A waiter brought fresh drinks to the table of Rowlandson, JT, and Betty.

Rowlandson flushed his finger in his drink, "I do not know why I come to these places. They are such bores."

Betty responded, "But these are your friends."

"Hah! Friends!" shouted Rolly. "Me lady, the only real friends a person has are his two little fingers."

He pointed at the fingers of his right hand.

"You see these little creatures?" He tenderly touched his fingertips.

"They are small and appear innocent enough, but they are the only friends I have."

He stood up, getting louder.

"They've been there when I needed them. When I am broke and thirsty, when I am down and out."

Rowlandson squeezed in closer to Betty.

"Why do you think all these people respect and honor me?

Because I am a great man? Hah! Why do princes and queens have me as their guest? These fingers. They are the reason."

Betty looked closely at the fingers.

Rowlandson said, "And for me, they are as much a curse as attribute."

John Bannister approached, "Is Rolly on one of his soap boxes again?"

He grabbed Rolly's arm, "Come on, Rolly. Let me buy you a drink and save your vocal cords for the day they hang you by them."

They laughed.

Rowlandson yelled, "That's right, Bannister. Let us have another round. In fact, let's have one for the house."

The entire room ran to the bar.

A fat little bar man ran up to Rowlandson.

He asked, "Mister Rowlandson, Please. I have enough paintings on my walls. I need money to run my business."

Rowlandson unfolded an easel.

"Do not fret, Samuel," he said. "I have money. But I shall not need it, for I am an inspired man and I shall paint you a fabulous masterpiece. You will thank me many times over."

The bar man held up his head, looking up. "Oh, my Lord, why me?"

The crowd drank loudly as Rowlandson began sketching.

Bannister said, "Rolly is such a character. He has played this trick on every innkeeper for a hundred miles."

JT asked, "Is he causing enemies?"

Bannister replied, "You must be joking. Those little sketches you see him drawing? They are his best kinds of work. And worth several times what this crowd can drink in a month."

Betty asked, "Why does he do it?"

Bannister said, "My dear. Thomas Rowlandson and I go

back many years, and I can honestly call him friend. But deep down inside, he is a monster, a gambler."

About an hour later, Samuel, the barkeep could be seen happy and in awe at the painting given to him by Rolly.

Rowlandson smiled as he walked up to Betty, JT, and Bannister.

"Forgive me for interrupting my good friends," he said.

They smiled at each other.

Rowlandson looked Betty in the eye, "May I have this dance?"

Betty said, "Why thank you very much."

They laughed together as they waltzed off to the dance floor.

JT spoke to Bannister, "Do you really think he is bad?"

Bannister put his arm around the lad, "Son, Rolly is not evil. Just too damn talented for his own good. He knows it, you know it, and I know it. And it will probably get him in trouble someday."

Rowlandson and Betty danced eye to eye.

He said, "You are quite beautiful."

"I am also quite engaged," she answered.

Rolly said, "I would not dream of interfering. JT is a special person."

Betty smiled, "Yes he is, and I don't want to see him hurt."

The old painter smiled facetiously, "Why, Miss Betty, I think you've fallen for me."

He quickened their pace, laughing all the way.

JT woke up the next morning, holding his head.

"Oh, my God, what a hangover."

He looked up to find himself surrounded by sleeping members of most of the same customers of the inn from the night before. They were all passed out.

JT said, "I wish I had some of Rolly's secret potion."

He began to look for Betty.

"Betty? Betty?"

He gazed at the many faces, but most were the faces of middle aged men.

JT walked slowly down a long hallway. A stranger came past him.

"Water, water," said JT.

The man pointed to a bucket.

"Look over there," said the man.

JT walked over to buckets of water and dipped his head straight in.

"Ooh, it feels good," he declared.

JT rubbed his head and shoulders with the water. As he dried himself off, he looked down the hall, noticing Betty coming out of a door.

Betty was settling her clothes onto her body and buttoning the top button to her dress.

She said, "Well, I will see you again, won't I?"

JT hid behind the corner.

Betty said, "Well, say something."

JT could see that the man Betty was talking to was Thomas Rowlandson.

Rowlandson said, "What do you want me to say? I love you? Yes, I love you my precious darling."

He was terrible at sarcasm. Betty's face turned red.

Rowlandson grabbed her. JT was getting real mad now.

Rowlandson said, "My dear, Betty. I really do care about you."

Betty sighed. They kissed.

Rowlandson asked, "Will you let me paint you?"

Betty answered, "Yes, of course."

Rolly said, "Alright, in the next week or two."

JT was upset. He was furious. But he could not get violent. He did not know why he could not kill the painter. He realized he could not.

JT watched Betty say goodbye to Rolly. She walked away. JT sat on the ground, shaking his head. Tears rolled down his cheeks.

~

Angelo's Fencing School.

JT acted crazy and angry.
"You think you are so great," yelled JT to Rolly.
Rolly embarrassed JT. He slapped him forcefully in the face. He quickly proved to be a master fencer, pushing JT to the ground.

~

Harry the bird chirped loudly.
Betty said, "The bird is adorable, isn't he?"
JT grumpily and sarcastically said, "yes, so adorable."

Rowlandson was sketching away. "Harry has done it again. My fingers are going so fast I do not know where they are leading. Only to success, money, and beautiful women."

Rowlandson laughed as he glanced over to Betty. JT fumed with anger.

"What does a bird know," said JT.

Rowlandson looked over to Betty, "what is his problem?"

Betty replied, "just a hangover."

Rowlandson looked to JT, "would you like a shot of our favorite potion?"

JT held his throbbing head. "No thanks. I am beginning to like this feeling."

Rowlandson's eyes locked on Betty's.

JT said, "oh, alright, just a sip."

JT guzzled a bit thrust of alcohol.

Rowlandson said to Betty, "our friend is angry."

JT yelled, "there is nothing wrong with me. Come

on, Rolly, show me how to draw like you do."

Rowlandson wiped his brushes, "I am not a teacher, Jay. But maybe when I return from Paris."

JT said, "Where are you going?"

Rowlandson answered, "Somewhere I can draw, and draw, and draw."

JT asked Betty, "are you going?'

Betty said, "Jay, I need to talk to you."

She grabbed his hand, leading him into the forest.

Rowlandson smiled. Betty and JT came upon a big rock.

Betty said, "What has gotten into you?"

JT replied, "Nothing."

Betty said, "Your nothings sure are something. Everything is so strange. Why can't things be easy?"

JT said, "All I know is that I love you. I love you more than ever."

She screamed, "things are so crazy. Jay, Rolly has asked me to go with him to Paris."

Jay's face turned blue.

"What happened to our being engaged?"

"I love you, Jay," she said. "I want you to know that. I am just a little confused inside."

She grabbed his arm, "please I know it is a lot to ask, but, please, please give me time."

He looked away.

Betty moved in front of him. "I have so many things going through my mind that, well, oh Jay, I do love you. Can't you understand?"

JT pulled away, "understand? I guess I am just the understanding type."

He looked at her close now.

"Betty, I understand you say you love me, but then I understand you want to leave me, even if only temporarily."

He looked to the sky now, "why should I understand?"

He looked to the beauty of Betty. She seemed so tender and cute.

JT said, "But all I have to do is to look at you and the sounds I hear in my heart tell me that everything will be alright."

Betty looks to JT. He touches her hair.

"I know I must be mad," he said. "But, go to Paris. Take your time you need. When you return, if you want me and if I want you . . ."

His eyes filled with tears. "Go, go to Paris."

Betty smiled. She kissed him. She did not know what to say.

Outside the forest, Rowlandson smiled as he drew a sketch of the rear of a group of pigs in a field.

Betty and Rolly took a ship across the water to Paris.

Betty grabbed her mouth, ready to puke.

Rolly kept his eyes to his canvas as he drew and sketched everything.

Betty looked out at the barren sea, with wind blowing through her hair.

Rolly sketched her and sketched her and sketched her.

That night he was in the pub, drawing sketches of all the people in the pub. Betty watched him draw and sketch, until in a passionate moment, Betty and Rolly embraced and kissed.

The next morning Betty woke up in a half empty bed. She slowly arose, walking over to another room. She found Rolly painting a landscape. She watched him silently. Rolly was totally engrossed in his art. He did not notice his audience.

Later that day, Betty was at a merchant, trying on

several beautiful dresses. She was surrounded by chambermaids.

"I hope Rolly likes it," she said.

The chambermaid said, "He should, madam."

Betty smiled, "let's hurry. I want him to see me in this gown."

~

It was a wonderful night. The casino was bright and cheerful. A carriage pulled up. Betty was helped out of the carriage.

The men gasped at her beauty. She was wearing a new expensive dress.

Inside the casino, Rolly laughed hysterically. He was surrounded by several French men. They were loud in their drinking and singing.

As Betty approached, the men became silent.

Rolly said, "Well, if it isn't my pretty little Betty."

She smiled, "Rolly, I wanted you to see my new dress."

"Isn't she so beautiful?" Rolled yelled.

The crowd cheered.

Rolly put the fabric of the dress between his fingers. "It is beautiful. How much did it cost?"

Betty said, "I do not know."

Rolly chuckled in a loud manner to the other men.

"She doesn't know."

He was getting sloppy in his drunkedness. He laughed closely in her face.

"Well, my dear, I have bad news."

Betty asked, "what are you talking about?"

Rolly talked to himself, "bad news, bad news, bad news."

Betty pulled away, "Rolly what is happening here?"

He laughed.

"You better sit down, my dear."

He pushed away the crowd of men to make room for his girlfriend.

"Come on, gentlemen, a chair please for the lady."

The gentlemen rose, diplomatically opening up a chair for Betty. She sat down slowly.

Rolly asked, "are you comfortable?"

Betty looked around at the faces of the gentlemen, then to Rolly.

"Tell me," she said.

Rolly slurred his words, "I hope you have money for that dress."

Betty replied, "Rolly, I used your name."

He laughed, "She used my name."

The crowd began to laugh hysterically.

Rolly said, "Betty, I just lost everything I own in the world in a game of chance."

He looked close at her, "can you believe it?"

He yelled, "I was this close to winning. But I lost."

Betty was stunned. Her face turned blue as she looked at the faces of the other men.

"What is the problem, Rolly," she said. "Just paint them something."

Rolly said, "stop the music."

The piano player stopped playing. There was dead silence in the room.

"What did you say?" Rolly asked.

Betty said, "you know what I mean. Your fingers. Remember? Just paint a masterpiece and everything will be alright."

Rolly yelled, "The lady is right. Bartender, it is drinks for the house, on me—Mister Thomas Rowlandson."

The crowd burst into cheers. Betty watched as Rolly laughed and laughed and laughed.

Rolly laughed and laughed and laughed. He was behind bars now, drawing a sketch.

He looked over to a fellow cell-mate, "Isn't this fantastic?"

His fingers moved slowly over the canvas.

"Peace, quiet, but not much fresh air. No Harry the Bird either. I wish Harry was here."

Betty was led through the doors of a jail. Her eyes were filled with tears. A lady of the night was with her.

"Don't worry yourself so, honey. This happens to the best of us."

Betty cried louder.

It was a sunny day. Thomas Rowlandson was being released. He walked past some gates until he could see the beautiful face of Betty. Under his arm were stacks of artwork.

He stopped to shake the hand of another convict. "It was nice meeting you, Jonathan."

He then shook the guard's hand.

"It was really nice meeting you, too.

He smiled upon seeing Betty.

"Betty, Betty. My dear Betty. Are you all right, my dear?"

He hugged her tightly.

Betty cried, "take me home. Please. I want to go home."

Rolly said, "I am sorry, my child. Of course, we shall sail the first ship to our home in England."

Outside of the British Museum, the streets were crowded full of people. A sign out front said, "British Museum, John T. Smith, Curator."

Inside the museum, JT spoke to a group of men, while looking over a drawing.

"Gentlemen, after consultation on my part with

the Prussian Embassy, I have been able to contract for this single piece. The only piece of artwork still alive from the entire Byzantine treasure."

The men whispered amongst themselves.

JT said, "and I must tell you that it shall be a worthy addition to the British Museum's collection of fine art."

The gentlemen applauded.

After the crowd dispersed, JT walked down a corridor, passing numerous paintings. He whistled all the way.

As he turned a corner, he saw Betty.

"Hello Jay" she said.

Jay smiled, "it has been a while."

She looked down at the ground, "yes, I know."

Jay looked at her beautiful hair and her beautiful skin. He asked, "Are you well?"

"Yes," she said, "I am. Thank you."

Jay asked, "and Rolly?"

She said, "I have not seen him in five months. He went on some painting expedition."

Jay said, "I read of his money problems."

Betty replied, "He gambled it all. All of it."

She began to cry. Jay held her.

"Betty."

She looked up, "Jay, you must hate me."

"I don't hate you."

"I would," she said.

Jay realized he was holding his dream girl.

"You are so beautiful," he said.

"Oh, Jay, I am so sorry."

They kissed hard until Jay's embrace completely enveloped Betty. Looking closely at her, he could see she was crying.

She whispered, "I feel so happy to see you, Jay."

She felt safe again in his arms.

A horse driven carriage hurried down the road. Inside the carriage Angelo and JT were talking.

"Thanks for coming with me, Angelo," said JT.

"Don't worry," answered Angelo. "Rolly is a pain in the ass most of the time but I imagine I still love him."

JT looked over to Angelo.

Angelo corrected himself, "as a friend."

They laughed.

JT said, "I read that Rolly is doing cartoons. Political cartoons."

"He has always been interested in politics," Angelo said, "but sometimes he does not know when he goes too far."

The carriage sped down the country road. It came up to Thomas Rowlandson, who was painting, as usual.

"My friends," yelled Rolly. "What brings you so far from the big city?"

Angelo said, "You, old man."

Rolly laughed.

Angelo hugged him, "we are your friends. We wondered how you were doing."

Rolly looked to JT, "how are you?"

Jay responded, "fine, and you?"

Rolly laughed, "I am a happy man."

"It is beautiful here," said JT.

"But too quiet," said Rolly.

JT looked up a tree, "where is your friend, Harry, the singing bird?"

"I have not seen him. Maybe he is dead. Maybe he has found another famous painter."

Angelo said, "Birds and painters. Always singing songs."

JT asked, "let us see your work, Rolly."

They walked over to the easel.

Rolly said, "It is nothing."

"Rolly," said Angelo, "I am glad to see you are painting again."

Rolly responded, "Angelo, you can stop your charade. Be honest. My so-called painting has not been much of anything lately. Some political cartoons of Napoleon and King you know who, but nothing that brings much as far as money is concerned."

Angelo said, "you put so much credence in money."

Rolly smiled, "I get thirsty, you know."

JT said, "It is too bad legends are titles made for the dead."

Looking up at a tree, Rolly said, "I wish Harry the bird would return. Sometimes I think that those songs he used to sing were my inspiration."

He panned across the trees, looking for the little bird.

"I started to sketch this two years ago and I have not had the vision or guts to finish it. Do you have a drink?"

JT and Angelo looked at each other.

Rolly said, "Perhaps I should break down and do the

paintings that people want. I was just offered one hundred pounds to do nude portraits. One hundred pounds.

JT screamed, "Dammit, Rolly. You are a great master. You do not need to do such things. Just paint what you see, what you feel."

Rolly said, "I am thirsty, Jay. I am thirsty."

~

The old man smiled with joy. He was holding a painting. He ran up to Rolly.

"Oh, Mister Rowlandson. I am very very happy. Here is your money. It is gorgeous. I cannot wait to see this above my fireplace.

The portrait was a nude woman.

Counting his money, Rolly said, "There are many more where that came from, Mister Thornton. Just let me know."

The man replied, "Oh, I will, I will."

Rowlandson took a sip of whiskey. He smiled as the man left. Rowlandson walked over to an easel, lightly touching it with a feather pen.

"I am an artist."

"I am a spokesman."

"I am a poet."

"I am a politician."

Rowlandson looked over to a large sketch he had made from years earlier. It was a painting of the Prince.

"Hello, Prince," said Rolly. "It has been a long time."

He was speaking to the portrait like it was a real person.

"Times have changed, haven't they?"

Rolly paced around the easel.

"You are no longer the Prince. Now you are King. Me, I am no longer a painter. Today I am a poet, a spokesman for the little people. The people who you spit on."

Sipping his whiskey, he continued. "I am also an

artist. And artists have no kings. We are alone. Our kings live in our hearts, our souls."

The portrait of the Prince seemed to smile. Rolly looked closer.

"But you would not understand. You are a powerful man."

Rolly sipped the whiskey.

"I am powerful, too. I can put you to your knees. I can and I will."

Rolly started laughing loudly. He began to draw madly.

"I can feel it. Harry the bird. You must be near. Help me. Help me not to lose it. I must not lose this fire in my blood. This anger in my head."

The sun was shining that morning at the British Museum.

JT looked over at a headline of a newspaper.

"Rowlandson is jailed by the King."

Angelo paced quickly around the room. In a chair nearby sat Bannister, nearly asleep.

"I do not believe it," said JT.

Angelo said, "He has gone and done it. 'The Brilliants'—what kind of title for a painting is that?"

Bannister said, "We knew he would do it. It was inevitable."

Angelo yelled, "Inevitable? We knew he was crazy. We knew he was a drunken, obnoxious fool, but did we know he would do something like this?"

JT said, "He is a painter. The greatest painter of our time."

Bannister shook his head, "a painter? He was a painter. Now he sketches nude women and draws for newspapers."

JT responded, "I thought you were his friend."

Angelo said, "Friend. We are his friends. What does it matter? Why? Why paint a picture of the king and queen nude? Why? Rolly, why would you do this?"

Bannister said, "I bet his paintings are worth more now. Just think of the publicity. I must work on this."

Betty and JT walked down the jail corridor. A singing voice could be heard echoing all the way.

JT said, "These places scare me."

"Brings back memories for me," said Betty.

JT said, "I hope he is all right."

"Rolly will survive, don't you worry," said Betty.

The singing got louder and louder. They finally could see Rowlandson in a cell, painting on an easel.

Rolly smiled, "Why if it isn't my two long friends Miss Winter and Mister John T Smith. What brings you down into the dungeon today? Oh yes, we mustn't forget."

He laughed, "Your friend has been detained."

He started yelling, "Jailed without consent. We must keep the local residents happy."

The other inmates started screaming and yelling. After a while the noise died down.

Rolly laughed, "Nothing like being famous, you know. I have been offered three files in cakes just this morning. It is crazy. You meet the nicest people sometimes."

JT and Betty looked at each other.

Betty yelled, "Is that all you can do? Sit and paint and make stupid jokes?"

Rolly smiled, "Betty you must not worry yourself so. I must say you are looking striking as usual."

JT stood between them.

"Jay," Rolly continued, "I have heard you are the lucky devil to have made this beautiful angel your wife. May I congratulate you?"

JT said, "Thank you Rolly."

Betty screamed, "Rolly, do you realize the mess you are in? The king wants to hang you. The queen wants you castrated."

Rolly said, "It feels great to be wanted."

Betty declared, "you are famous. Is that what you want?"

She pulled at her own hair in anger.

"Rolly, you don't need to do these things. You ARE famous. You were before all this. You are a great painter. Why paint something like 'The Brilliants'?"

Rolly stopped painted for a moment. He said, "what do they want?"

JT said, "All you have to do is apologize."

Rolly answered, "for what? And make myself out the crazed idiot who drank his mind away? Never. I'd soon rot in hell than apologize. I painted that man's portrait as he wanted then and I painted it as I wanted now. What is so wrong? It is only a painting."

Betty shouted, "But nude, Rolly. You painted the King and Queen nude."

Rolly asked, "It is the way I see them. A good effect, hey? Tell me, can you get me some liquor? I need liquor."

Betty grabbed JT's arm.

"Let's go, JT. We are getting nowhere."

As they began to leave, JT said, "Don't worry, Rolly. The fame you want is here. Right now. Your painting 'The Brilliants' is the most talked about art piece in the world. Are you happy?"

Betty pulled JT away, out to the corridor.

As they went down the corridor, JT looked back and saw his friend Thomas Rowlandson smiling, whistling, and painting.

"Kill For Love"

It was a snowy day as numerous shoppers walked up and down the icy sidewalks, carrying bulky packages.

Through the manifold crowds, a song was heard being sung by a group of carolers. They were young, heavily dressed children.

"City sidewalks, dressed in holiday style, in the air there's a feeling of Christmas."

Veva, a thin, dark-haired woman of twenty-seven, pushed her way, as if in a daze. Looking tired and weary, her face had streaks of mascara running from her bloodshot eyes. As she moved her way through the crowds, everyone seemed happy but her.

A sign said, "Seattle General Hospital."

Veva walked slowly, bumping into people. She passed an old man dressed in a Santa Claus suit who was ringing a bell.

"Ho, ho, ho! Merry Christmas! Merry Christmas!"

Veva ignored him as she approached the emergency entrance.

She entered the crowded room. It was decorated for the holidays, with a large Christmas tree standing at one end.

Veva was quiet as she glanced at the many people sitting everywhere.

At one end, a woman held a crying baby. At the other stood a long line of people waiting to see a doctor or anyone who could ease their pain.

Veva walked over to the back of the line. The room seemed quiet and melancholy except for some Christmas music, which blared, from an old man's portable radio.

Finally Veva reached the front of the line. A nurse shuffled through a pile of paperwork.

"Can I help you?"

Veva answered, "Uh, I'm not feeling too well."

The nurse looked down at the papers.

She said, "Well, don't feel like the lone ranger. The holidays bring out the worst in us all."

Her eyes looked up at Veva. "You look like you haven't slept in a while."

Veva put her hand to her hair, "My head hurts really bad."

The nurse said, "Well, you just fill these forms and I'll get someone to look at you in a couple of minutes."

The mean woman handed Veva a stack of papers and a pen.

Veva walked over toward a chair. She looked straight up at the sky as she suddenly collapsed onto the floor, unconscious.

For a moment she laid there, unnoticed, until a little boy finally saw her.

"Mommy, look at that lady!"

The mother screamed, "Oh my god! Nurse! Nurse!"

People crowded around the body.

A woman from the crowd yelled, "I know that lady! She's Veva King! She is the wife of the Mayor!"

Several nurses and orderlies broke though the crowd.

It seemed like hours later.

In a small, dark room, Veva lay, eyes-closed on a bed. Looking over her was a silver-haired man, Doctor Barker, staff psychiatrist for Seattle General. Also in the room stood two husky men in pin-striped suits.

Veva seemed frozen.

Her silent body began to come to life. Slowly her eyes started to open.

Everything appeared fuzzy. Slowly she began to focus in to Dr. Barker's face.

"Mrs. King," said the doctor.

Veva asked, "Where am I? Who are you?"

"My name is Doctor Barker, Mrs. King. You've been sleeping a long time."

Veva looked over to the two big guys next to the wall.

She yelled to the big guys, "What do you want from me?"

The doctor told the men, "You had better go."

The blonde-haired big guy responded, "Our orders are to protect Mrs. King, and that's exactly what we're going to do!"

Veva asked, "Protect me from what?"

He got mad, "Listen to me." He put his face up close to the big guys.

"Get the hell out of here! You can wait outside her door."

The big guys looked to each other, shrugged, and then headed toward the door.

The doctor was surprised at their reaction.

The blonde big guy said, "We'll be right out here if you should need us, Mrs. King."

He closed the door behind him. Doctor Barker looked over to Veva.

"Mrs. King."

Veva looked up to him. "And I suppose the TV and newspaper guys are out there, too."

The doctor asked, "TV and newspaper guys?"

"Yeah, this must have made the front page and the six o'clock news."

She smiled, sat up, and glanced across the barren room.

The doctor said, "Mrs. King, we've been in touch with your husband, and . . ."

"Charlie? Oh, no! I won't see him."

The doctor leaned down to her, "But, Mrs. King."

She jumped up, "Tell him to leave me alone! Please, doctor, do I have to see him?"

Barker looked closely to her. Veva seemed terrified as she crouched under the bed sheets.

Outside of the room, the two big guys sat in chairs in front of the door.

Barker came out through the door, briskly walking toward the nurse's station. The blonde big guy followed him.

"Doctor, how is she?"

Barker spoke to a woman, "Nurse, can you please call my office and tell them to cancel all my appointments the rest of the day."

"Yes, doctor."

The big guy said, "Doctor."

Barker responded, "You and your fellow ape over there can situate yourselves outside Mrs. King's room. No one is to see her without my personal approval, do you understand?"

The big guy said, "Listen, doc, sorry about the screaming in there, it's just that this is a very sensitive situation we have here."

The doctor replied, "No problem. You do your job, I'll do mine. Just stay out of my way and we'll get along just fine."

The blonde big man said, "There will be some reporters here in a few minutes."

"Mrs. King is not to have any interruptions, understand?"

The big man nodded, "Yes, sir."

Barker headed back to the room.

The elevator door opened. Out came several new reporters and cameramen. They stampeded at the big men.

"Oh, Shit!" said the big guy.

Inside the hospital room, Veva was lying quietly on the bed. Barker sat on a chair next to her, writing on a pad of paper.

"Now, I want you to just relax, Mrs. King. No one is going to hurt you."

"But," she said.

The doctor replied, "Just lie there and tell me everything from the beginning."

Veva looked around the room. "There's nothing to talk about, doctor. I'm okay, nothing is wrong."

The doctor asked, "Then why are you here??"

"I, uh, don't know," she answered.

"Mrs. King."

"Call me Veva."

"Okay, Veva, you haven't slept in days. You are paranoid. The only way I'm going to be able to help you is for you to be honest with me and tell me everything."

Veva squinted her eyes.

"Okay."

The doctor prodded her, "Okay, now let's start at the beginning."

Veva said, "Beginning? You want to know about everything from the beginning?"

She looked at her fingernails. "Shit, when did it all start? I guess everything started seven or eight years ago. Yeah, just before I was to graduate from college. Mom and Dad took me and my sister Betty on a trip to Tahiti for a Christmas present."

~

It was a very sunny day in Tahiti. Like a picture postcard, the beaches were filled with beautiful girls running joyously through the sand.

Veva and her younger sister Betty walked down the sandy beach. They carried small light rafts.

Both of the girls were bikini-clad, with Veva looking young, happy, and clean.

Veva said, "Betty, this is going to be great! Just look at how blue the water is."

Betty looked around the beach. "Who cares about the water? Look at all those gorgeous looking men!"

Veva smiled, "I can't wait to see everyone's faces back in Seattle when I go back with a beautiful, dark tan, and in January."

"I'd rather go back with some great stories to tell," laughed Betty.

Veva pointed, "Let's lay out over there next to that rock. I bet the water's warm."

They carried their rafts over to the water next to a rock. After a few moments of putting on suntan oil, they drifted out onto the water. Their eyes were closed. They baked in the sunshine, but it felt great.

Betty asked, "Veva, do you think we'll get lucky and meet some rich, handsome me?"

Veva smiled, "Betty, we're out here to just take it easy. Besides, mom told me to make sure you stay away from boys. Ha, ha."

"Why does mom always treat me like a baby? Sometimes I think she's trying to turn me into a nun or something."

Veva laughed, "Don't worry. I've got a gut feeling that Tahiti will be good to us."

A fast, bright-colored jet-ski boat sped across the coral bay. It was pulling Charlie, a tall, lean, but muscular man of forty-nine, on water skis. He smiled, and then looked over to the shore.

In the distance Veva and Betty could be seen lying on the rafts.

Charlie signaled the boat driver to take him towards the girls.

Betty said, "All I want is to find myself a gentleman. He doesn't have to be great looking, as long as he's got lots of money and treats me like a lady."

Veva felt the sun's rays on her brow. "Dream on. Men are all the same. They've all got just one thing on their minds."

Betty opened her eyes.

"What's that? Sex?"

Veva said, "I wish! All they're interested in is themselves."

"Veva, that's a hell of an attitude."

Veva sat up, "You'll learn soon enough."

Betty said, "I just want a man that is distinguished. Like Cary Grant or a prince.

Veva said, "Betty, I think sometimes that you watch too many movies."

"That's right. I want a prince who's got it all. Good looking, rich, debonair."

The boat hurtled toward the rafts. It turned sharply, swinging Charlie at them. He dropped his ski-ropes and skied up to the girls.

Waves from the boat toppled Veva off her raft and into the water.

Veva yelled, "Oh! Ahh!"

Betty and Charlie laughed. Veva was soaked from head to toe and not taking it so funny. Charlie noticed her lack of humor and made a straight face himself.

"Sorry about that," he said.

He picked her up into his arms and walked up onto the

beach. Veva seemed angry. She took a moment to look this stranger up and down.

"Uhm, you can put me down now."

Charlie said, "Oh, yes of course."

He put her down.

Betty approached, giggling, "Veva, are you all right?"

Veva answered, "You're a big help."

Charlie picked up a towel off the ground. He put it around Veva.

"Here you are. My name is Charlie, by the way. Uh, I'm sorry. I hope I didn't hurt you."

Veva dried herself. "No, I guess not."

Betty smiled at Charlie. "Oh, she's okay. Uh, she's Veva and I'm Betty. We're on vacation from Seattle, Washington."

Charlie shook her hand. "Well, I'm pleased to meet you, Betty, Veva. It's nice to meet some fellow Americans so far away from home."

He asked Veva, "I hope you'll give me a chance to redeem myself."

"I don't know," she said.

Betty jumped in, "How about dinner at the Tahiti Club, tonight, say six o'clock?"

Charlie said, "That would be great."

He looked over to Veva. "What do you think?"

Veva nodded, "Oh, okay. We'll meet you out front."

A horn beep was heard from the ski boat. The ski boat driver was getting impatient.

Charlie said, "I've got to be going. It's nice meeting you both and I'll see you at six, okay?"

The girls shook their heads with acknowledgment. Charlie gave them a salute with his index finger, and then nervously walked back into the water. There he picked up his ski and looked to the girls as he put it on. Veva dried herself as he skied off into the distance.

Betty said, "What a doll."

Veva dropped the towel to the ground as they started back down the beach with their rafts.

Betty asked, "How come you get all of the luck? He could have knocked me over."

Veva said, "He's alright."

"Alright? Don't you know who that was?"

Veva said, "No, who?"

"I don't believe it. That was Charlie King!"

"Who?"

"Charlie King! He's just one of the big leaders of the Independent Party, the mayor of Seattle, and the most eligible bachelor in the state of Washington."

Veva looked to Betty. She was speechless, her face flushed. She watched in the distance as the ski boat left them.

A couple of boys ran by them, toward a crowd that had gathered up ahead.

Betty said, "I wonder what's going on up there."

Veva answered, "Let's go find out."

They ran up to the crowd. Tony, a good-looking, strongly built, young man of twenty-three, was instructing a scuba class.

He said, "In underwater recovery work, a scuba team usually drops from a fixed surface point and searches the immediate bottom, making sure that all the area is covered, until the object of the search is recovered."

Veva was mesmerized by Tony. She stared at his muscles.

After a moment, Tony seemed to notice her glances.

"Uhm, these are the same techniques used by air to sea rescue teams, and in this work . . ."

He began to lose his concentration as his eyes started to fix upon Veva's. After a few moments of silence, a student faked a cough.

Tony continued, "Oh, in air to sea rescues, an aircraft is used to start from the last known . . . and, uh . . .

Veva smiled.

Tony said, "You people seem to need some brushing up on this subject. Re-read chapter six and seven for tomorrow. You will be tested on them. Class dismissed."

The students sighed like they wished he would continue.

After a while, the crowd dispersed. Some giggles were heard from the students, who glanced towards Veva. Tony approached her.

"Hi, my name is Tony."

"Veva. My name is Veva Carter."

Betty watched as these two people locked eyes.

She said, "I, uh, think I hear someone calling me. Veva, I'll see you later. Do you hear me, Veva? I'll see you later, at dinner at six, remember?"

Veva shook her head yes. Tony smiled at Veva.

"Can I offer you a drink?"

Veva said, "I don't mind if you do."

Inside the Paradise lounge, many young tourists danced to a loud rock group which was situated at one end of the bar. The room was dark and smoky, allowing it's patrons some privacy under the quiet roar of music.

In a booth, Veva and Tony sat very close to each other. They laughed. A waitress arrived with drinks.

Veva smiled as she looked at Tony.

Tony eyed Veva as he signed the waitress' notepad.

Veva said, "Nice place."

Tony said, "Yeah, my father does alright with this place."

"Your father owns this?"

"Yes, he started it a few years back. I come down here and do those scuba classes whenever I can get a break from Berkeley."

She asked, "Berkeley? It must be crazy out there with

all those demonstrations I keep hearing about."

"Crazy? You call crazy, people trying to stop a war forced upon them by barbaric old men who sit behind their big corporations and drink scotch?"

Veva said, "I didn't mean . . ."

Tony was upset, "Crazy? People who are against dying in a war that hasn't even been declared? You . . ."

"Tony!"

Tony stopped his monologue.

"I'm sorry. Sometimes I lose my cool."

Veva said, "No problem. There's nothing wrong with caring."

He smiled.

"Do you know you have a cute nose?"

They laughed. The rock band started playing a song.

Veva said, "Come on. Let's dance."

She led him by the hand onto the dance floor.

They danced cheek to cheek. Veva enjoyed herself, as they constantly glazed into each other's eyes.

Later, inside Tony's apartment, the room was pitch black. Some keys could be heard jiggling from the door. The door opened, spraying a silhouette of light across the room.

Tony and Veva entered, turning on lights as they went. They laughed hysterically.

Tony said, "So the guy opens the lid and says, 'I drank the whole thing?' ha, ha, ha."

Veva laughed so hard that she almost cried. They sat on the couch. Veva looked around the room. It was full of expensive French antiques and plush furniture.

"Not too shabby."

"My father takes good care of me. Most of this furniture is direct from Paris, where I was born."

Veva walked around closely examining the antiques. Tony went to a desk drawer and pulled out a plastic bag.

"Go ahead and put on some music."

He pointed to an elaborate fidelity sound system. Veva walked over to it and flipped through several record albums that were leaning on a shelf.

She read the album covers, "Janis Joplin, Louis Armstrong, The Who, Beatles, Frank Sinatra."

She looked over to Tony, who was rolling a marijuana cigarette.

"Pretty versatile music for a radical scuba diving teacher, isn't it?"

Tony took a smoke from the cigarette. As the Sinatra music began, he approached her. He handed her the cigarette.

"So, I'm a radical, huh? Why is it that anyone who doesn't conform to the middle class's standards is called a radical?"

"This is pretty good pot."

"It should be for fifty bucks a lid."

Tony put his arm around her. Veva took a hit off the joint.

"God, I have a low tolerance."

Tony asked, "Know something?"

"What?"

Tony pulled her tight, "When I look in your eyes I get a chill up my spine."

Veva smiled. They kissed. He tightened his hold on her, when she suddenly pulled away.

She went to the couch and took another drag off the cigarette.

She said, "I could use a drink."

Tony was disappointed, but shook his head, okay. He walked into the kitchen and opened the refrigerator.

Veva said, "You know, I can remember the first time I ever smoked pot. Can you?"

Tony came in from the kitchen carrying a couple of beers.

"I don't know, it seems I've been smoking it all my life," he said.

He sat down next to her. Veva watched him as he popped off the top of the beer.

She said, "The first time for me was with some friends—I guess you could call them friends. I was in my first year of college. The room was so dark, the music so loud. The Beatles. God, how they could sing. Strawberry Fields Forever. Boy, What an awakening."

Tony said, "Still can."

"What?" She wondered.

"They still sing great."

He put down the cigarette and moved closer to her. He took the beer from her hand and put it on the table.

"You know something?"

Veva smiled as he got closer.

"What?"

Tony said, "I knew it the first time I saw you."

"What's that?"

"Your eyes, they sparkle."

"Sparkle?"

"Yes, there's an old French myth that says a sparkle in the eye of a beautiful woman means one thing."

Veva smiled. "What's it mean?"

He said, "It means that she is in love."

He pulled her to him. They kissed, passionately and long.

"Whoa!"

Their embrace got stronger, their breathing heavier. Veva's eyes closed.

Suddenly a loud gonging was heard. Veva's eyes opened to see a large clock on the wall. It said six o'clock.

Charlie looked at her. She yelled, "Oh, Shit!"

"What is the matter?" he asked.

"I was supposed to meet somebody at six," she said.

Tony kissed her neck.

"What could be more important than this?"

Veva tried to resist his kissing, but her breathing got

heavier as his lips touched hers.

"Oh . . . oh . . . oh."

Over at the Tahiti Club, Charlie stood in front of the club, with Betty. He was dressed in a tuxedo. He looked at his watch, laughed, and shook his head. Betty and Charlie entered the club.

Back at Tony's apartment, Veva said, "Oh what the hell."

Veva and Tony rolled on the ground, grabbing at each other's clothing.

"Mrs. King . . ."

Back at the hospital room, Dr. Barker looked at Veva who had closed her eyes.

"Mrs. King," he said.

Veva opened her eyes.

"Oh, I guess I was getting a little carried away."

"It appears that your experience in Tahiti was a real important one for you."

Veva nodded, "It sure was. I had never met a guy like Tony before. And it also was the day I met Charlie for the first time, even though

I didn't get off on the best foot."

"When did you see Charlie, Mister King next?"

Veva closed her eyes.

She was transformed to many years ago. She was in a basement tunnel at a giant political convention.

A large mob rushed through the tunnel. The mob is made up of mostly very young people, and led by an exuberant Charlie King.

The mob screamed, "King! King! King!"

Veva opened her eyes. She told the doctor, "About a month later, my father took me with him to a political convention. How did I know that the star of the show was to be none other than Charlie King, my famous water-skiing friend I stoop up in Tahiti?"

She closed her eyes to see a black and white television set.

Frankie Shore, a television reporter, spoke to the camera.

"This is Frankie Shore on location at the Independent

Party Convention, where Charlie Elliot King has just been chosen their party leader. Using the widely publicized campaign slogan "Realist with Dreams", Mister King has captured the imagination and enthusiasm of this convention hall."

The crowd roared.

Charlie led the crowd through the tunnel.

Veva stood at the end of the tunnel, next to her father.

Her father said, "A most impressive showing."

She smiled. "A most impressive man."

Charlie recognized Veva. He rushed over and kissed her on the cheeks.

The mob pushed him away from her. He looked back desperately through the crowd.

Veva was stunned. Her face blushed as she watched him being pulled away.

Reporters surrounded Veva. They began a barrage of questions.

"Miss, are you a girlfriend of King?"

"How long have you known him?"

"Have you eyes for King?"

"Are you lovers?"

Veva was dumbfounded by all of the attention. She hesitated.

"My name is Veva Carter. I am only a college student. I have eyes for him only as mayor."

The reporters sighed, then rushed off after the crowd.

The lone reporter, Shore, slowly follows them, but looked back to Veva with curiosity.

She stood silently next to her father.

Veva opened her eyes. Doctor Barker wrote in his notebook.

She said, "I wasn't lying either. Little did I know how much things can change."

Hands applauded. Veva was at her graduation. She smiled as she accepted her diploma.

"Well, a couple of months passed, and I was lucky to graduate from college. As a reward for my patience, my parents offered me an all expense-paid trip to wherever I wanted to go."

College students threw rocks at national guardsmen who were wearing gasmasks, hitting people with their billy-clubs.

"Tony was back in Berkeley working on a peaceful anti-Vietnam rally, and I was thinking about paying him a surprise visit, but a friend of mine, Amy, invited me to go with her and a couple of her friends on a trip to wild and crazy Morocco."

A 747-jetangeeer landed with a screech of its tires.

"I just couldn't turn down an offer like that, so the next thing I knew I was landing in Marrakech, looking forward to my first trip away from my parents."

The jet taxied down the runway. It pulled up to the main terminal and stopped.

Veva walked down the stairs of the jet, followed by several other young people dressed in the hippy-styles.

A Chevy station wagon slowly made its way through the jam-packed roads. Street merchants strenuously pushed at the windows.

Inside a station wagon was Veva, Amy (a good-looking girl of twenty-two), and many other young men and women sitting very close, singing folk songs. One guy smoked a joint and passed it along. Everyone swayed to the music.

It was a hot day. A trail of dust silhouetted the path the station wagon took across the desert.

The station wagon pulled up in front of a village of huts and tents. Everyone jumped out with enthusiasm.

Veva looked around at the blue sky, squinting as the dust settled. Amy ran up, smiling.

"Well, Veva, what do you think?"

Veva yelled, "This is going to be great!"

Amy screamed, "You bet your life it's going to be great. Veva, every little urchin in every rat hole in the world would kill for a trip like this, and here we are."

"I can't believe I'm really here."

Amy looked over her shoulder to the others who were entering the huts. She lowered her voice to Veva.

"Veva, I can guarantee you one thing. This is going to be one trip you'll never forget."

They laughed. As they approached the huts, the music got real loud.

Amy said, "Come on."

She pushed aside a dark curtain that acted as the front door to one of the tents.

Inside the tent, people were lying all over the place. Some were embraced, kissing, others were just staring as if in trance.

Loud rock music blasted from an old record player on the table. A couple of young girls started dancing. The room became smoky. It was lit by several candles positioned around the perimeters and among the mangle of bodies.

Veva was mesmerized by what she saw. She looked over to Amy who was rocking to the music.

A man walked up to Amy. He kissed her. They embraced tightly for a moment and then he walked away. He carried a large bottle of whiskey.

Veva watched like she was watching a movie, not real life. She seemed stunned.

"Who was that?"

Amy responded, "Hell if I know."

"You mean you've never seen him before?"

"Come on, Veva. Relax. We've come five thousand miles for a good time. Loosen up."

Amy put her arm around Veva. They giggled.

In a corner, a man played his guitar. Some of the others joined in, singing.

A man and a woman cuddled tightly, kissing, as if in a world all their own.

The party got wild.

Veva took a swig from a whiskey bottle. The dancing got crazy. Everyone in the crowd was laughing hysterically. Veva kissed one man, than another. People began to snort cocaine on mirrors.

Some of the women began to take off their shirts. This led to more kissing.

Veva snorted cocaine through a tightly wound One Hundred Dollar Bill. Then she laughed. She looked around the room. A girl smoked pot.

As the music took over her mind, everything became fuzzy.

Veva was still. Her eyes were closed. Slowly her eyes began to move.

She discovered herself to be in the middle of a heap of naked bodies.

"Oh, my head," she said.

She raised her hand to her head, tied her gown to her body, and maneuvered herself across the bodies.

As she slowly climbed over people, she could see the faces, but they were unrecognizable.

"Amy? Amy? Jesus, what's going on?"

Veva came out of the desert hut. She had tears in her eyes. She looked around. The station wagon was the same way they left it the day prior. She walked over to it and sat onto its bumper.

She asked herself, "What the fuck have I done? Why am I here?"

She held her head. Not far from her she could see an old truck, which was being worked on by a long-haired Arabic man. Veva was happy to see a living soul. She approached him.

"Sir? Have you seen my friend Amy?"

The man said, "Que? No comprende, senorita."

"Shit," she said.

Veva went to the station wagon and back onto the bumper.

"What am I? What the hell am I doing in this God-forsaken place. Oh shit!"

She began to vomit.

The Arabic man turned toward her, shaking his head.

~

It was just after dawn on the dusty road. The sky was a beautiful shade of purple as the sun began to rise above the distant mountains.

Headlights.

A truck moved up the road. It pulled over at a crest of a hill and the passenger door opened.

Veva got out, holding a suitcase. Inside. the man spoke something in Arabic.

Veva answered, "Thanks. Shit, you can't understand me anyway. Uh, gracious."

She waved the car on. Her face was dusty and dry. She looked around, up and down the road, but it was empty and deserted.

She felt alone.

"Why me? Why do these things always happen to me?"

She walked slowly down the road, holding her finger out to the few cars that passed by.

The streets were busting in the morning sun in Marrakech.

An old bus pushed its way through the crowds.

The bus door opened. Out came a weary-looking Veva, carrying her suitcase. She looked as if she hasn't had any sleep or a shower in days.

A beggar grabbed at the suitcase handle. Veva pushed him away.

"Hey! What are you doing?"

She pulled at her suitcase and started running. She was terrified and startled by the street vendors and persistent beggars as she squeezed her way.

The crowd tightened its squeeze on her, when a hand grabbed her hand, pulling her from the crowd, into an alley.

She could see that the hand belonged to a young Arab boy.

"Let go of me," she yelled.

The boy said, "Pretty lady, you must watch out for crowds like that."

Veva said, "What are you talking about?"

The boy said, "This town is full of men looking for pretty ladies like you."

"What for?"

"Take."

"Take?"

The boy asked, "Never you heard of white slaves?"

Veva pulled back, "Oh, no! Here?"

"You must watch yourself, pretty lady. Lady like you brings many francs."

Veva said, "The embassy. Where's the American embassy?"

"Follow me." The boy said.

Veva hesitated. She looked at him. He looked back at her.

"Okay," she said.

The boy led her through dark alleys, around corners, and through torn down buildings.

"Are you sure you know where you're going?"

The boy said, "Follow."

After a while, they arrived at a room full of young people. The boy let go of her hand. He walked to a white man. Veva noticed he said something undetectable. The man looked over to Veva, shook his head. Suddenly the boy ran desperately out of the room.

Veva yelled, "Hey, where are you going?"

The man approached her.

"Come with me," he said.

Veva answered, "Who are you? Where are you taking me?"

"You have nothing to worry about," he said.

"Do you have a name?"

The man smiled, "Whitlow, James Whitlow."

"American."

The man took her through broken, crushed rooms.

He said, "We're from all over the world. Looking for a place to hide, go cold turkey, to live."

A drug addict lay on a mattress. His whole body trembled, shaking and screaming.

"They call it tripping. I call it hell," the man said.

Veva watched closely, horrified.

"Can't you do something?"

The man answered, "I already have. He has a roof over his head and that's my mattress he's lying on."

"A real bleeding heart."

The man grabbed her arm tightly.

"Listen, lady, this isn't no picnic. AWOLs, junkies, deserters, pimps. They call it the flower generation, well I call it the hell generation."

Veva said, "Just tell me where the American embassy is and I'll get out of your way, okay?"

"In time."

Veva lay on a mattress.

She told herself, "This is hell. Here I am in the middle of a strange country lying on a strange bed, not knowing what to do. The man promised to take me to the embassy the next morning, but, oh, how the time was going so slow.

She tried to get comfortable, but she kept tossing and turning. Her frustration level was high. She felt claustrophobic.

A scroungy degenerate peaked his head around the corner, eyeing Veva.

Veva was looking the other way. Suddenly the man jumped onto her. He grabbed at her clothing.

She screamed, waking up many others around her, but they just stood back and watched. Many of the bystanders seemed to be enjoying the show.

Veva clawed the man in the face. The man yelled in pain.

Veva got away from his hold for a moment.

The bloody face off the man was coming at her. He was real mad, now.

Suddenly the room began to shake. It was an earthquake.

Veva was startled. The bum started panicking. Veva ran out of the room, down stairs, and into the street.

There was extreme panic in the streets. The earth shook and shook. Buildings fell all around Veva. She ran speedily, constantly asking directions to the embassy.

Bricks from a building fell onto her, knocking her unconscious.

Her eyes were closed.

Veva awoke to the sounds of crying babies. Her head was bandaged.

Everything seemed fuzzy. Slowly her eyes slowly focused in to a nun's face.

"Where am I? What happened?"

The nun said, "Don't try to talk, my dear. You've been through a lot. Earthquake and all."

Veva tried to get up, but she felt quite a pain in her head.

"Oh, my head!"

The nun said, "Sleep, just sleep."

~

Inside a 747 jet, Veva sat next to a window, staring dazedly. There was a bandage on her forehead.

"I had had enough of Morocco. All I could think of was Tony and how much I loved and missed him. Before I knew it, I was in a jet headed straight for Berkeley. Boy, was Tony going to be surprised."

The streets of Berkeley.

Veva drove a red Volkswagen. She stopped every

once in a while to ask for directions.

She came to the door of an apartment. Veva felt excited as she rang the doorbell. The door opened.

"Tony!"

Tony looked at her with surprise.

"Veva!"

They embraced. Veva kissed him hard.

Tony said, "Veva, what a surprise."

Veva smiled, "I knew you'd be happy. Well, aren't you going to invite me in?"

"What? Oh, yeah. Sure, come in. I'm sorry."

He brought her inside his apartment.

Tony said, "Well, sit down. Can I get you anything? A coke, or something?"

"No," said Veva. "I'm fine, Tony."

They sat down on a couch. Veva smiled brilliantly. She could not hold herself back. She kissed him again.

"Oh, Tony, I can't tell you how much I, uh, it's been a long time."

Tony said, "It sure has."

Veva looked around the room. "This is a nice place."

"It's okay," he said.

"You wouldn't believe what happened to me in Morocco."

Tony said, "Yes, I would."

Veva screamed, "It was just horrible. There was this earthquake, and this man tried to rape me, and I had a bad trip with some dope, and . . ."

Tony looked distracted. "Sounds like a real soap opera."

Veva said, "Oh, I'm just so glad to be here with you."

She embraced him tightly. He was not very enthusiastic.

"You know, Tony, after all that, the only thing I could think of was you."

Tony was surprised, "Really?"

"I, uh, I've really been doing some thinking," she said.

She tried to embrace him again.

"I've been thinking about you. You and me."

Tony said, "Oh, yeah?"

"Yes, and I, uh, think I'm finally ready to settle down."

Tony was startled. He pulled away.

"What are you talking about?"

Veva said, "You know."

Tony shook his head, "No, Veva, I don't."

"Well," she said. "I was thinking about Tahiti and, well, I just thought that you and me, well, you know, could have some babies."

Tony stood up, arms to his hips. "Now hold it just one minute!"

He grabbed her hand, "Veva, come with me. I've got something I want to show you."

He led her though the apartment, up the stairs to a back bedroom.

The room was very small with a bed on one side. The walls were plastered with posters of Malcolm X, Chairman Mao, and Abbie Hoffman.

Veva looked over to the bed, where she could see numerous machine guns, grenades, ammo, and more posters.

"Tony."

"Veva, you're living in a dream world. Just like all the other middle class idiots who think life is just a bowl of Wheaties, a bottle of Pepsi, and Walter Cronkite on the six o'clock news."

Veva asked, "Tony, what are you talking about?"

"Veva," he answered. "You're beautiful, and all that."

"So?"

He said, "Times have changed. We've tried to do things the hard way, the peaceful way. But nothing happens. Nothing ever happens. Well, now something is going to happen. Now we're going to do something that will really get their attention."

Veva cried, "I can't believe this is happening."

He yelled, "You better, because it is."

He looked down at her sad face.

"Veva, why don't you get out of here. You heard me, come back when you've learned something about the real world."

Outside again, Veva sprinted to her Volkswagen. Once inside, she put her head into her hands and cried.

It felt safe on the back porch of Grandmother's house.

Veva spread out on a lounge chair looking out to beautiful bluffs, full of evergreen trees.

She read a book entitled, "Medium is the Message" by Marshall McLuhan.

"I stayed at my grandmother's house near Seattle for it seems a long time. I was trying to get my head back together. I was like a hermit. I didn't talk or see anyone, not even my parents. My heart ached like it never ever did before, or even since. I guess it was the first time I had ever been turned down."

Veva put the book down for a moment. She looked out to the trees and over to a group of birds. The birds were building a nest not far from her.

Inside the house, a phone rang.

Grandmother opened up the back door. She said, "Veva, your mother is on the phone, dear."

Veva said, "Grannie, I told you I didn't want to talk to anyone right now."

"She says its important."

Veva went inside.

"What could be so important?"

She walked inside and grabbed the receiver off the table.

"Hello, mother."

"Veva?"

"Mother, how are you?"

"Veva, an old boyfriend of yours just called, wanting to take you out on a date."

"Mother, I told you, I don't want to see anyone!"

"But, Veva, he seems like a real nice fellow. You must remember him. From Tahiti?"

"Tony. Mother, I don't care who it is."

"But, Veva, he's the Mayor, Charlie King!"

Veva did not say a word.

"Hello? Veva? Are you still there?"

Veva started thinking about shopping. She remembered feeling exuberant.

She loved trying on flashy new dresses in prestigious boutique shops, new shoes from classy shops.

She loved getting her hair permed and her fingernails manicured.

She loved the way she felt when she was shopping.

~

Veva's father loved playing the piano.

Veva's father played and sang a song.

Veva watched her father trying to entertain the family.

She felt surrounded by her four sisters.

Patty, Kellie, Angee, and Betty.

They ran about, helping Veva with her dress, hair, and makeup. They giggled.

Veva said, "I can't believe this is happening."

Patty replied, "Neither can we."

The girls kept uncontrollably giggling.

Veva said, "I haven't seen Dad that happy in a long time."

Angee said, "It's not everyday that one of his

daughters goes out on a date with the Mayor."

Betty shouted, "And a handsome one at that. You should have seen how he was looking at Veva that day in Tahiti!"

Patty remarked, "Do you think he'll try anything on the first date?"

Kellie answered, "I don't know, but I saw in the newspaper a picture of him dancing with some real beautiful American actresses."

Veva yelled, "Won't you please let me worry about that! I'm the one going on the date."

They laughed loudly. Veva's mother came into the room.

"Veva's right. I'm sure that she is old enough by now to get ready for her date by herself."

The girls sighed, then burst out laughing again.

The doorbell started ringing. Everyone, including the parents, rushed to the door.

Veva said, "Hold it!"

The family stopped. They looked around to her.

She said, "I thought I was the one going on this date?"

They were silent. Slowly they smiled.

Mother said, "She's right. Everyone, let's go sit down and act like normal. James, you go back and start playing something; girls, pick up a book and start reading."

The family raced to their spots. Veva smiled. She took a big breath.

The door opened. There was Veva, all dressed up.

"Hello."

The streets of Seattle were wet and colorful. The bright green colors from the stop lights reflected off the wet black streets.

A black limousine drove past.

Inside the limo, Veva and Charlie smiled nervously. Veva looked around at the sophisticated communications, a wet bar, and a television set that were all around them.

Veva said, "Nice car."

Charlie said, "Goes with the job. Uh, you look very nice, Veva."

"Thanks, you do too," she said.

Veva looked to the front seat of the car, where Harry and Claude, the husky bodyguards were sitting.

Charlie laughed, "Don't mind them, they go with the job, too."

Veva answered, "Look, I'd like to apologize about Tahiti."

Charlie tried to stop her, "You have nothing to apologize for."

Veva was firm, "Yes I do. I stood you up and I want to let you know how embarrassed and sorry I am."

He smiled. "Veva, I went to Tahiti with the intentions of reading a book, "The Rise and Fall of the Roman Empire," and to decide whether or not I should run for Mayor again. I achieved those goals on that trip and I was and am satisfied. You needn't apologize because you are young and, well, let's forget the past and just concentrate on tonight, okay?"

He smiled.
Veva said, "Okay."

Inside the restaurant, tuxedoed waiters carried trays full of steaming dishes to tables full of couples who looked out on balconies to the city lights of Seattle. Veva and Charlie sat at a small table with Harry and Claude not far away at a table of their own.

Charlie mentioned, "This place isn't too bad."

Veva said, "It's very nice."

"So, tell me," he said. "What have you been doing since Tahiti?"

She sipped a glass of wine. "Oh, I've been keeping real busy. After I saw you I graduated from college, took a vacation overseas, and have been lately doing some research on a book."

"A book? That's great. When you were overseas where did you go?"

They seemed happy together.

Veva said, "Oh, the usual. Europe, Africa."

Charlie looked up to the moonlight coming in from a window. "I love to travel. It's the best way to educate ones self. After I graduated college some years back, I went to Europe and hitchhiked over most of the entire continent. It took me almost seven years."

She asked, "That must have really been a great experience."

He replied, "It was probably the best years of my life. As far as your book, which is it, fiction or non-fiction?"

Veva's face turned red, hesitating.

"I'm sorry," she said.

"What's the matter?" He asked.

"I have a knack of making a fool of myself. I didn't go to Europe and there's no book. I guess I'm afraid of . . ."

He grabbed her arm. "There's no need to feel ashamed."

She said, "You haven't heard my story yet."

"You don't have to tell me if you don't want to," he replied.

Veva was surprised at Charlie's sincerity.

"No, for some reason I want to tell you."

He refilled her glass.

"Here, try a glass of wine."

He held her hand over her glass.

Veva smiled, "thanks. Well, I graduated alright. No lies there, but I traveled not to Europe but to Morocco."

"A beautiful country."

She said, "I went with some of my college friends to, well, what you could probably call a commune. You know, full of sex and drugs. That sort of thing. Are you sure you want to hear this?"

Charlie listened intently, "Veva, we've all got war stories to tell."

Veva said, "I didn't realize what I had gotten myself into until it was too late, and I, uh, kind of made a fool of myself."

Charlie replied, "We all do that sometimes."

Veva smiled. She couldn't believe he was listening to her.

"Sometimes it seems like I get more than my share. After I left the commune I stayed at a halfway house run by some Europeans and Americans. That's when I was almost raped."

Charlie was stern. "You're kidding?"

"But before the earthquake saved me," she said.

"Earthquake?" he asked.

"That's how I got into the hospital," she answered.

Charlie said, "Veva, I think that perhaps you should change your mind about that book. It sounds like you have plenty of fuel for a real juicy bestseller."

"I don't know if anyone would believe it," she said.

They laughed. Charlie put his hand onto hers. Veva looked into his eyes. She smiled.

A voice said, "Mister Mayor?"

A tourist couple approached.

Charlie answered, "Yes?"

"Can we get a picture?"

Charlie looked to Veva. She was flustered.

Charlie said, "Sure, go ahead."

The man took a flashed picture.

Other patrons saw the flash and looked toward Charlie's table. Suddenly they crowded around them.

Veva was angered by the people's rudeness.

Harry and Claude rushed to them and broke up the crowd.

Harry said, "Okay, let's break it up."

The crowd yelled, "OOOOOOHHHHHH."

Claude replied, "You heard the man. Let's let the Mayor enjoy his meal, too."

Harry said, "I'm sorry, sir."

Charlie nodded, "That's okay."

Charlie was smiling. Veva was not.

She said, "I cannot believe how rude some people can be."

"Such is life in politics, Veva. Most people are nice though."

Veva leered to the patrons who stared at them.

She said, "Do they always stare?"

Charlie said, "Just for a few minutes. Come on, let's dance."

"You can really take things in stride, can't you?"

"Politics, remember?"

He led her to the dance floor, where other couples were already joined in a slow dance.

Veva and Charlie held each other closely as they danced smoothly.

Charlie said, "You know, I'm old enough to be your father."

She replied, "So?"

"Does it bother you?" he said.

She pulled away a little, "Come on, let's just enjoy our selves and worry about it all later, okay?"

Charlie smiled, "Okay, you talked me into it."

He pulled her closely to him as they danced with ease.

The black limousine pulled up to the big house. Harry jumped out of the right front passenger door and opened the back one. Out came Charlie and Veva.

Charlie motioned to Harry, "Go ahead and pull the car up a little."

Harry replied, "Yes sir."

The car pulled away. Charlie looked over to Veva, who was grinning.

"Well, Veva," he said.

"I had a marvelous time."

She nodded, "So did I. Charlie, thank you."

Charlie put his arm around her.

"Veva, all of your experiences. Morocco, everything. They are just a part of growing up."

"Sounds like lecture time," she said.

He responded, "Sorry."

She laughed, "I'm kidding."

Charlie said, "What I meant is that you should put these experiences to good use."

"What do you mean?"

"Become an actress," he said, "or write that book. Do something. Move East. There's nothing but opportunity there and especially for someone like you."

Veva said, "Someone like me?"

"You know what I mean," he replied. "And if you ever get out to Seattle give me a call. I'll promise you a nice free dinner, okay?"

She exclaimed, "You don't know what you might be getting yourself into."

They laughed. Charlie embraced and kissed her lightly.

It was dark inside the Carter house. Veva entered, closed the door, and leaned against it. She sighed.

"Seattle, here I come."

The car was moving fast.

Veva drove speedily down a highway in her Volkswagen. She was wearing large sunglasses, her hair blowing in the wind.

She could see the incredible skyline of the city of Seattle.

The year was 1969.

Veva kept busy trying to get a job and an apartment.

She entered a building that had a sign: EMPLOYMENT AGENCY.

Veva took a typing test, then found herself shaking hands with her new employer.

Veva red the newspaper classified. She circled the paper classification, APARTMENTS FOR RENT.

Veva shook her head no at first one apartment, then another, and another, until finally she was shaking her head affirmatively, she found the right apartment.

Inside her new apartment, Veva stared at the telephone.

She told herself, "It took me two weeks before I could build up enough courage to even call Charlie."

She started dialing a number.

"By this time I was convinced he wouldn't even remember my name."

Charlie was in his office when the phone rang.

"Veva! You're in Seattle? Great!"

Veva said, "Charlie! It's so good to talk to you."

"I want to keep my promise," he said. "How about joining me for dinner tomorrow night. Yes? Wonderful. My men will pick you up at six. Be warned, though, it's only spaghetti."

Veva jumped up and down on her bed. Her face turned red with joy. Suddenly the bed broke.

It was dark that night in Seattle. A long black limousine sped by.

Inside the backseat of the limo sat Veva. She looked around inside the car. She could see the highly technical communications equipment, a wet bar, and the color television set.

Veva was intrigued by it all.

She looked to the front of the car where Harry and Claude sit.

Harry looked back at her and said, "Make yourself comfortable, Miss Carter. We should be arriving at the Mayor's Mansion in just a few minutes."

Veva was quiet but nervous as she smiled at him.

The car pulled up to the front gate of the mansion, where a security man spoke to Claude. The car then went down a circular driveway to the front entrance to the mansion.

Harry opened the door for Veva. She got out, but was stopped by a group of men in pin-striped suits. One of them approaches her.

"Good evening, Miss Carter," he said. "My name is George, inspector for security. If you would please excuse the inconvenience, could we please examine your purse?"

Veva said, "Uhm, sure, I guess."

"There's nothing to worry about," he replied. "Just procedure."

While he looked through the purse, another of the men held a buzzing metal detector around Veva's body. George seemed satisfied with his search of the purse. He handed it back to her.

"Thank you, Miss Carter. We appreciate your cooperation."

The men broke apart, allowing Veva to approach the front door. Before she could knock or ring the bell, the door opened. A maid looked up to her.

"Follow me, please."

The maid led Veva down a long corridor and into a room that appeared to be a study or office of some kind.

"The Mayor will be down shortly."

Veva said, "Thank you very much."

The maid left the room.

Veva looked around the room to find it filled with numerous elegant antiques, paintings, and sculptures.

She noticed several pictures and photographs of Charlie with heads of states, show business celebrities, and other world leaders.

Veva stopped at a large King campaign poster. The poster showed Charlie in front of a large political rally. At the top of the poster, in large, bold letters, were the words LA RAISON AVANT LA PASSION.

"La raison avant la passion," she said.

"What a ham I am."

Veva turned around to see Charlie's smiling face.

She said, "Charlie!"

"Veva!"

She kissed him lightly as they embraced.

The candles were flickering in the dining room. Veva and Charlie were seated, eating dinner and drinking wine.

She said, "and so I decided what the hell, I got into my Volkswagen, and, well, here I am."

Charlie grinned, "Very impulsive, but I'm glad. Have you plans? A place to stay?"

"Don't worry," she said. "I've already gotten a job and an apartment. So I guess whether you like it or not you're going to probably be seeing more of this young girl."

Charlie was surprised, but he smiled.

"I think you will do alright for yourself, Veva."

She said, "You're the one who invited me."

He laughed, "I'm glad you've taken my advice. Now maybe you can write that book you were talking about, or do whatever you want."

They smiled. He put his hand onto hers.

That evening Veva and Charlie walked hand in hand through a park next to a river.

"Such a beautiful night," she said.

He looked at her big eyes, "I jog this way every morning. It keeps me in touch with life. The trees, birds, and just plain old clean air."

Veva answered, "There's nothing like the cold morning air to wake you up. Charlie, that poster in your study. The one that says, "La Raison Avant . . ."

Charlie nodded, ""La Passion." It's an old motto of mine, from where I studied Aristotle in Paris."

"What does it mean?" she asked.

"Reason before passion. My whole life I have studied history, and so many times have the people's lives been manipulated by passionate, unreasonable men. Napoleon, Hitler, others. I think Aristotle was right. Those who govern must use reason before passion. I pray to God that I will."

Veva put her arms around him as they leaned on a rail of a bridge that overlooked the river. The moonlight was reflecting brilliantly off the water.

She said, "This all seems so unreal. One minute it's rallies, conventions, mansions, bodyguards, reporters, and then the next it's peace and quiet of a forest and moonlight on an open bay."

He whispered, "Life is rich. I cannot think of anything I treasure more than the outdoors and beauty of this country and her people. Especially when I'm blessed with the company of a beautiful woman. Thank you, Veva."

"For what?"

"For tonight. For your beauty, your vitality, your youth. You make me feel regenerated."

She said, "Shoot, you probably say that to all the girls."

They chuckled. Charlie looked her in the eyes and kissed her. Veva had a sparkle in her eye.

The next morning, Veva hummed a happy tune.

She was lying on her bed in her apartment. She stared at the ceiling. The doorbell rang.

She got up off the bed, and walked over to the door. A young delivery boy was holding a box.

"Flowers for Miss Carter."

"I'm Miss Carter."

"Sign here."

Veva signed the boy's slip and closed the door. She hurriedly took the box over to a table. She was anxiously smiling.

"Roses!"

She opened a little envelope that sat on the flowers.

She said, "Thank you for last night. It was fun and wonderful seeing you again. I'll be in touch. Love, Charlie."

Veva was touched. She sighed.

Again the doorbell rang.

"I can't believe it."

She opened the door to see a mailman.

"Certified letter for Veva Carter."

"I'm Veva Carter."

"Sign here, please."

She signed the man's pad and closed the door behind her.

"Letter? I wonder who it could be from."

She looked down at the letter. Her face turned from happy to shock.

The return address said, "TONY LEWIS, BERKELEY, CALIFORNIA"

"Tony?"

She ripped open the envelope. She started reading the handwritten letter. A tear ran down her cheek.

Doctor Barker said, "What did he say in the letter?"

Veva said, "I couldn't believe it. After that episode in Berkeley, he had the gall to propose to me!"

The doctor said, "Propose? As in marriage?"

Veva said, "Well, not in those words, exactly, but he said he was sorry and that he wanted me to go with him on a trip around the world in a sailboat."

She wiped away her tear, sat down, and started to write a letter of her own.

The doctor asked, "What did you do?"

"I wrote him back. I told him thanks but no thanks. I told him he was too late."

"How did you feel?" asked the doctor.

She said, "Pretty damn good. He had his chance."

Veva sealed the envelope, put a stamp on it, and went over to her roses. She put them into a vase. Her sad face relaxed into a happy one again. She took a rosebud over to a mirror.

She smiled as she gently hugged the rose to her cheek.

"For once in my life I had made a decision and nothing was going to get in my way. Nothing. Not even an old heartthrob."

Inside the nightclub a waiter carried a tray full of plates.

Veva and Charlie were dancing cheek to cheek.

"Charlie and I started seeing each other more and more until we got consistently to two dates a week."

Charlie said, "Do you realize that I'm old enough to be your father?"

She laughed, "You don't feel like my father."

The pulled each other closer in their dance.

Charlie and Veva locked into a tight and passionate kissing embrace.

Charlie and Veva skied down a mountain.

"Veva," he said. "I am much too old for you."

Charlie kissed Veva.

Charlie and Veva went to a rock concert.

"I'm old enough to be your father," he said.

Charlie kissed Veva.

Charlie and Veva went to see a foreign film.

"I'm a little bit old for you," he said.

Charlie kissed Veva.

Charlie and Veva loved dancing close. Charlie perspired heavily.

"Am I too old for you?"

Veva smiled. He kissed her passionately.

Charlie looked at himself in a mirror.

"What's happening to me? I'm old enough to be her father. Then why do I feel as I do? Look at me. I'm a grown man. Mayor of Seattle. I'm supposed to know better. Reason before passion, remember?"

His forehead had beads of sweat forming on it.

Veva looked at herself in the mirror, talking to herself.

"I think he likes me. I know I like him. He makes me feel good. Like no one I've ever met. Is it serious? What's he thinking? It's all happening so fast. Is it love? I think he likes me."

She smiled.

Charlie stared right at the telephone. He looked nervous. He picked up the receiver and started to dial, but half way into the number he put it back down.

Veva stared right at the telephone. She looked nervous. She picked up the receiver and dialed the operator.

"Operator? This is 555-3344, could you please call me back. I think my phone must be out of order."

She waited. Suddenly the phone rang. Veva's face lit up.

"Hello? Oh, thank you, operator, thanks for checking my phone. Yes I am expecting an important phone call."

She slowly put the receiver down.

Veva watched TV. Every few seconds her eyes darted over to the silent telephone.

Veva played solitaire. She looked over to the silent telephone. She threw the cards up into the air.

Veva and her mother walked down the sidewalk, carrying packages.

Her mother said, "I'm happy you were able to get away and visit me, Veva."

"I am too, Mother," she answered. "Let's go have some coffee. Over at that café, okay?"

"Sure."

They entered a café.

Veva and her mother drank some coffee.

Veva said, "And I just don't know what to do. He hasn't called me in weeks. Maybe he's getting cold feet."

Her mother said, "Have you called him?"

"I'v wanted to, many times, Mother," she said. "All the time, but I'm not the one who is going to crawl to him."

"Veva, don't let this turn into something more than it already has. This isn't war."

Veva pulled out a newspaper from her purse.

"I wasn't too upset. Well, maybe a little, but look at this."

The newspaper showed a picture of Charlie out dining with Barbara Streisand.

"It's not the first one, either," declared Veva.

Her mother responded, "Veva, calm down. Charlie is probably a little scared. It's natural. All men get scared. Your father did, you grandfather did, they all do."

"They do?"

"Sure they do," Mother said. "The best thing to do is to just wait. If he loves you everything will work out. Have a little patience."

"I've never been too good at patience," Veva said.

"It's all you can do for now."

Veva said, "Come on, mother. What happened to my favorite matchmaker? Don't you have any dirty tricks?"

"Don't worry, you won't need any. You must remember that Charlie is a very important man. He's got tremendous responsibilities to many people. He's probably very nervous right now. So give him some room. If it's right, and I think it is, he'll be back. Have patience."

Veva smiled. She hugged her mother.

"I hope you're right, Mother. Thanks."

~

Helicopters flew through the jungle, American GI's crawled through the swamps. It was a network TV newscast showing activity from the Vietnam War. A South Vietnamese general pointed his revolver to a Viet Cong's head at point blank range and pulled the trigger right in front of the camera.

Walter Cronkite said, "And that's the way it is." Veva was watching her TV set, very shocked at the horror she just saw. The phone rang. She walked over to the phone, still with her eyes glued to the set.

"Hello?"

Charlie said, "Veva, how are you?"

The phone was silent.

"Veva, are you there?"

"Yes, I'm here."

Charlie said, "Veva, I'm going on a trip to the San Juan Islands this weekend, and I was wondering if you could join me."

"You've really got a nerve," she said. "You know what? Why me? Why not take one of your actresses?"

Charlie said, "Veva, I know you're mad and all that, but I've got to see you."

She said, "What for, more pain?"

"I know your upset."

"Upset? Me, upset? Charlie, I can't go on playing these games."

"Veva, I've done some serious thinking. I've got to talk to you. Come with me to the San Juan Islands. Please?"

The phone was silent.

Charlie said, "Please? We'll have time to talk."

"Okay."

Charlie said, "Great! I'll pick you up at six."

Veva smiled.

~

It was a beautiful day on the island. The sun shined through the bright blue sky.

Harry and Claude watched as Charlie and Veva sat at a pier, talking.

Charlie said, "Veva, I, uh . . ."

He looked to her. He saw her smile. He looked over to the sandy beach where a few children were playing, and then back to her.

"I have been doing a lot of thinking lately, and, uh . . ." Veva said, "And . . ."

He said, "Do you know how old I am?"

"Yes, I do. You're over fifty, so what?"

"Veva, I'm old enough to be your father."

"Charlie, I don't care how old you are."

"I don't know," He said.

Veva said, "All I care is that I love you."

Charlie swished a stick in the water. He glanced to the kids on the beach and then back to Veva.

"Veva, what do you think about children?"

"I love 'em," she said.

He said, "These past few days I've really been doing a lot of thinking about a lot of things, and, I'm not getting any younger."

"I love you," said Veva.

"I want children."

"Yes."

"I guess maybe we should talk about getting married."

Veva's eyes lit up.

She jumped onto Charlie, causing them to both tumble into the water. Veva screamed and splashed with joy.

"When? Tomorrow?" She yelled.

Charlie laughed. He pulled himself out of the water and helped her out, too.

"Hey, take it easy," he said. "You must realize that you are not marrying just anybody."

Veva had tears in her eyes as they embraced.

Everything became a blur for Veva.

Over the next few days, Veva and Charlie were very close as they walked through the forests, along the beaches, having a good time fishing, skin diving, and kissing.

Inside the cabin one night, the room was totally dark but for the flickering of the fireplace.

Veva and Charlie cuddled up in a blanket, sipping champagne. Charlie kissed her.

"Veva," he began, like he was making a speech. "I love you and I want to marry you very much, but we can't forget my responsibilities. I'm Mayor. We've got to make sure everything is right, okay? I need for you to do something that I know will be hard, but it's something that must be done. I need for you to tell me everything about your past. EVERYTHING!"

Nodding her head in agreement, Veva said, "Charlie, I understand. No matter what happens I know that you will always have priorities."

He smiled, "Thanks, Veva. I must know everything about your past in case someone ever tries to blackmail me. There are people out there who will do anything. I must know where I stand. No surprises, okay?"

Veva became quiet. She was apprehensive.

"Okay, where do you want me to start?"

Charlie grinned.

Over the next few hours, Veva told him everything about her life. The good, the bad, and the worse.

Veva finally finished her story.

"And, well, you know the rest."

Charlie was sullen.

Veva said, "Charlie, is everything okay?"

"Just that I know you'll leave me someday."

"No!" she yelled. "I won't! I won't!"

Charlie glanced at her silently. "Thank you for being honest," he said.

She asked, "Does it change anything?"

"No," he replied. "I know how I feel. I love you, and that's all that matters. I still fear the age differences. I know you will go someday, that's all."

She stood up, yelling, "What am I supposed to say? I'm sorry?"

"No. But there are going to have to be some conditions for this marriage."

"Conditions? Real romantic."

"You must be faithful," he said.

"I love you!"

"I understand," he said. "But it's not going to be easy for you. Being the wife of the Mayor is a rough job."

Veva declared, "You won't have anything to worry about, I promise."

Charlie looked her in the eye, "No drugs. I cannot have my wife, the wife of the Mayor, stoned out of her mind."

"There will be no problem," she said. "Anything else?"

Charlie smiled, "I won't have a circus wedding. It must be quiet and a secret."

Veva responded, "Secret? Charlie, I've dreamt of my wedding day all my life, and you want it to be a secret."

"You cannot tell anyone," he said. "Until we are sure. No one, not even your friends or family."

"Not even my family?"

He said, "When we are ready, okay?"

Veva's eyes filled with tears.

"Anything you say" she said.

Charlie grabbed her, "Veva, I love you. I just have to be sure."

He kissed her.

~

Veva sat with her family, laughing in the Carter house.

"And so I went and lived with my parents in Seattle. I never thought I could keep it all a secret, but I was bound and determined to succeed."

Veva practiced learning French with the other students.

"Charlie was a master of many languages, his favorite being French, but I was only a speaker of English. So while I was waiting to become his wife, I decided I would surprise him and learn French, and . . ."

Inside the Catholic Church, Veva knelt in front of a priest.

"And by becoming a Roman Catholic."

Charlie and Veva kissed. Stopping for air, Charlie said, "Okay, let's do it."

Veva gasped for joy.

Veva sat in the bedroom, looking in the mirror. She was trying on her wedding dress. She looked at her sisters around her, giggling.

Betty said, "I cannot believe it."

Patty added, "My sister marrying the Mayor."

Kellied yelled, "And a handsome man at that."

Angee said, "Veva, aren't you scared to death?"

Veva smiled, "I guess it hasn't hit me yet."

The phone rang. It was her mother.

Veva's mother cried. She picked up the phone.

"Hello?"

Back at a radio station, a disc jockey spoke into a phone.

"Yeah, this is Tommy Lewis from KTL RADIO-AM. I'm trying to confirm a rumor that's going around that one of the Carter girls is marrying a diplomat or high government official. Is there any truth to this rumor?"

Veva's mother smiled to the phone, "Ha, ha. God, I wish it were true. No I'm sorry, none of my daughters is getting married."

Inside a radio station control room, the disc jockey shook his head, "Okay, sorry for the trouble."

Inside a chapel, an old lady played the organ wedding march as Veva walked down the aisle, her arm held by her proud, crying father.

Charlie waited for her, a very happy man.

Charlie and Veva knelt before the priest.

The priest bowed his head, speaking Latin.

Veva smiled brilliantly. Her eyes began to wander. She looked over to Charlie, who, eyes-closed, was in the midst of a prayer. Veva looked at the priest, at a bouquet of roses, and then back to Charlie.

"The most important day in my life," she told herself, "and I can't stand still."

The priest said, "Do you take this bride to be your lawful wedded wife?"

Charlie replied, "I DO."

The priest looked to Veva, "Do you take this man to be your lawfully wedded husband?"

Veva looked to Charlie, Saying "Oui."

Charlie was surprised at her French. He was quite pleased.

"You may kiss the bride," the priest said.

Veva had tears running down her face as they embraced and kissed.

Veva and Charlie exited the Chapel to a barrage of rice being thrown by both families. They jumped into a limousine, Veva and Charlie cuddling as they waved good-bye to all. A driver piloted them away.

"Finally I was it. The epitome of everything I ever wanted to be."

~~~

The snow was bright white at the ski resort.

Veva and Charlie skied quickly down some slopes, followed by several security men who fell down a lot.

Veva said, "Well, for our honeymoon, we went on a trip to the ski slopes, without even the slightest leak to the press. Of course, with us came our entourage of security people, I was to have to get used to. I bet it surprised a lot of people when they heard that I, Veva Carter, was to be the new first lady of Seattle."
~~~

Several headlines from newspapers all over the world announced the surprise marriage of King, Seattle Mayor, to a very young mystery woman, Veva Carter.

A TV reporter said, "The shock of the world came today with the announced marriage of Mayor Charlie King to a twenty year old Seattle woman, Veva Carter. Who is this new first lady of Seattle?

A still photo of Veva appeared.

"Daughter of former Secretary of fisheries, James Carter, the Mrs. King is a graduate of Simon Fraser University. The question in everyone's minds is: How will this beautiful young twenty year old bride handle her new role as wife of the most important elected official in Washington?

A black limousine pulled up to the Governor's mansion. Veva and Charlie jumped out of the car, cuddling like long time lovers.

Charlie said, "Well, Veva, uh, Mrs. King, we are home at last."

Veva laughed, "I hope I can make you happy, Charlie."

"I already am," he replied.

They entered the house, arm in arm.

Inside the mansion, Veva said, "Everything is so fantastic. Has it hit you yet?"

Charlie nodded, "It probably won't hit us for a while, but I'll probably be too busy to realize it."

"Busy?"

"I'm sorry, Veva," Charlie responded, "but the job of Mayor doesn't stop for weddings, funerals, or much anything else.

"I know," she frowned.

She looked around at her new home.

"I'm going to make this place the best home a Mayor ever had."

Veva oversaw the redecoration of the entire mansion. Rolls and rolls of carpeting were brought in and laid.

Many walls were repainted, much new furniture bought, and most of the rooms were rearranged. During this time, Charlie was busy at work in his study, on the road making speeches, and very much wrapped up in his work. Veva seemed very enthused and happy with her work.

In the dining room, Veva and Charlie sat for dinner.

Veva said, "And the rest of the furniture should be here by the end of the week."

Charlie replied, "That's great, Veva. One thing is for sure. I've been eating a lot better now that I'm no longer a bachelor."

Veva grinned, "I just have been working with your kitchen staff on making sure your diet is more balanced, that's all."

"Well," Charlie responded, "I think you're doing great.

How's it going for you? Do you like being subjected to protocol and etiquette that goes with your job?"

"I don't care what it takes, as long as you are happy."

Charlie held her hand. A servant walked up and handed Charlie a note.

"Thank you."

The servant exited as Charlie read the note.

"Everything okay?"

Charlie looked stunned by what he read.

"Why? Why him? Jesus!"

Charlie walked into his study and picked up a phone. Veva followed in behind him.

"What's the matter, Charlie?"

Speaking into the phone, "When? No, we cannot give in. You know me. Why ask those kinds of questions. Okay, but keep me posted. Okay. Thank you."

He slammed down the receiver, looked over to Veva,

and approached her. He put his arm around her.

"What's going on?" she asked.

Charlie said, "Two groups of gangsters have kidnapped a member of my City council."

"Which one?"

Charlie said, "Abraham."

Veva shrieked, "Oh, no. He's one of your best friends."

"Yes."

Veva asked, "What are you going to do?"

"I have no choice. Veva, my whole life I have been a man of principle, one of which is that we should never negotiate with gangsters or terrorists."

"A realist with dreams or a dreamer with reality."

"Exactly. Even though Abraham is one of my best friends, I cannot make any deals to save him. These people are gangsters and terrorists. Veva, if it was you, or a baby of ours, my decision would have to be the same. No deals, no amnesty. Can you understand that?"

Veva asked, "You mean that you would let them kill me, rather than to agree to terms?"

"Yes. Yes, I would. Veva, I'm Mayor. My duty to my office must come first, no matter what the circumstances. It's not morally right to give in to fanatics whose declared aim is to overthrow the system through violence and terror. Once you do that, you're lost."

Veva replied, "What are you going to do?"

Charlie said, "All we can do is wait, and pray."

He hugged her.

Later that night, in the middle of the night, the room was totally dark.

A phone rang. A few moans of waking up were heard. Charlie turned on the light next to the bed, picking up the receiver of the phone. Veva sat up and rubbed her eyes.

Charlie spoke into the phone, "Yeah? Oh, my God! Where did they find him?"

He quietly put down the receiver. Veva didn't say a word. Charlie had tears running down his face. He cried. Veva put her arms around him, trying to comfort him.

"I tried to comfort him. Abraham was dead. I knew that my strength was in my innocence, my ignorance of politics. I couldn't understand the political implications, but I could love him. That night brought us very close together."

Veva had a tear running down her cheek.

"Charlie was a shaken man. It was as if Abraham's death lay on his shoulders alone. He was the one who wouldn't negotiate, he was the one that was responsible. I don't think

I've ever loved Charlie more than at that moment."

~

The dance hall was full of happy people. Veva and Charlie danced vibrantly at a large Easter ball. At the end of the song another man asked her for the next dance. While they danced, Veva thought, "Well, things went pretty good for Charlie and I. We were the life of the parties."

Veva loved dancing.

"Then something wild happened."

Veva fainted, causing a scare into the crowd. Charlie rushed up to her, picking her up into his arms. He took her to a back bedroom where he put her onto the bed.

"Veva," he whispered.

A man pushes his way through the crowd to Charlie.

"Sir, I'm a doctor."

"Great. What could it be doctor?"

"Why don't you and all the others please give me some room. Please wait outside, okay?"

"Sure, okay." Charlie faded back. He told everyone to please go back to the party.

~

At a hallway at the hospital, Charlie paced up one way and down the other. The door opened. Out came the doctor.

"Mr. King, you can come in now."

They entered the room. Veva was sitting up on the bed.

Charlie asked, "Veva, are you alright?"

The doctor said, "She's fine. Just a fainting spell."

Veva was quiet.

Charlie was impatient, "Is there anything wrong, Veva?"

Veva smiled.

"The doctor says he's got to take some test to be

sure, but all the symptoms suggest . . ."

Charlie said, "Symptoms? What is it, doc?"

"Mr. King, I'll need to make some tests to be sure, but I would guess your wife to be approximately four to six weeks pregnant."

Charlie was speechless. He looked to his smiling Veva, who shook her head affirmatively. Charlie embraced her with tears running down his face.

A photographer set up his equipment for a family portrait of the King family. Veva was there with Charlie, who was holding their baby boy.

"Charlie always had a standing joke that he was keeping me barefoot and pregnant. Well, God blessed us with three beautiful and healthy sons, two of them born a year apart on Christmas day."

Charlie loved holding a child, while Veva rocked another child.

Like in a dream as the years past, so grew the people in the photograph. Eventually Charlie held a child, Veva held a child and the oldest boy stood next to them.

A large jetliner took off.

"I always knew that the quiet days of home life couldn't last for long. Charlie wanted to expand his work into international arenas, so we set out to visit most of the great countries of the entire planet."

Charlie, Veva, and the kids visited with heads of states from everywhere. Famous people like Willy Brandt, Chou En Li, Jimmy Carter, to Israel's Begin, and Russia's Brezhnev.

"We truly enjoyed ourselves, but I really found a rude awakening when it came to the press and the media. It seemed like I was always getting into trouble."

Newspaper headlines said:

VEVA KING WEARS MINI DRESS TO WHITE HOUSE

SEATTLE'S FIRST LADY DISGRACES HOME TOWN

VEVA MAKES WORST DRESSED LIST

VEVA KING IS TOO YOUNG

"A lot of what they were saying was true. Sure, I was new at being the Mayor's wife, but I was doing my best."

Inside their private jet, Charlie was busy reading legislation. Veva sat next to him looking out the window. She looked down to a newspaper that sat on her lap. It had a large headline that read: VEVA KING EMBARASSES SEATTLE.

Veva looked at the headline, frustrated. "I can't believe it," she said.

Charlie consoled her, "You shouldn't let it bother you."

Veva was sad, "Charlie, I'm sorry if I cause you so much trouble."

He held her hand, "Veva, you're my wife. I don't care what the papers write or what anyone says. I love you, and besides, they do the same things to Mrs. Nixon, Mrs. Castro, and every Mrs. Head of State, Mrs. New York City, and Mrs. Chicago in the world.

"You think so?"

"Of course."

"Thanks," she said as she gave him a big hug.

Charlie said, "Now, I've got to finish reading these business papers before we get to Seattle. Why don't you go back and visit our press corps, after all, what a better way to get some good press than by letting them get to know you?"

Veva looked at him curiously.

"Maybe you're right, you know, that's exactly what I'm going to do. All right!"

She got up out of her seat and walked through a door to a back section of the plane, where the news correspondents hung out.

The reporters were laughing and taking swigs from large bottles of rum, whiskey, and scotch.

Veva was taken back by their boozing and jollity.

The reporters straightened up a little at the sight of Mrs. King. That is, most of them, except for a few who noticeably have had a few too many.

"Ah, if it isn't Mrs. King," a drunk reporter yelled.

"Cool it," said another reporter to the drunk.

"Good morning, Mrs. King."

Veva approached them, "Good morning, everyone."

She sat down among them.

One reporter piped up immediately, "Is there anything we can do for you, Mrs. King?"

Veva answered, "Well, I was hoping we could just sit and talk for a while. It seems that sometimes you members of the press and I misunderstand each other. And I thought that perhaps we could develop a better dialogue, so that these misunderstandings don't happen in the future."

The reporters laughed and sat up straight in their seats.

"Mrs. King, I hope you realize that we don't mean you any harm. We're just doing our jobs."

Another reporter added, "That's right, Mrs. King. We don't mean you any harm."

The drunk reporter said, "I'll tell you one thing, we haven't had a field day on anyone like you in a long time."

"Don't mind him."

The drunk laughed, "Yeah, don't mind me."

Another correspondent said, "Mrs. King, I thought that song you sang in Caracas was nice."

Veva smiled, "You guys sure gave me a lot of flack on it."

Everyone laughed.

"Yeah, I guess we did. But you've got to remember. You're news. And we know that you're okay. It's just that what you say and do sells newspapers. Just like that song you sang. It was nice and sincere, alright, but we've never seen the wife of the mayor sing a song before, that's all. We don't mean any harm."

Veva chuckled with them.

The drunk said, "How about singing that song for us?"

Veva looked around. The crowd was all smiles in anticipation.

"Well," she said, "I don't know."

A journalist asked, "Come on, you're among friends."

The drunk yelled, "Yeah!"

The drunk started a small semi-hidden tape recorder.

Veva said, "Well, okay."

She started softly singing the song.

The reporters enjoy the song, as they passed around their bottles of liquor. They each took a swig from the bottles. One reporter handed the bottle of rum to Veva as she sang. She looked around at the reporters, who all smile innocently. After a second of hesitation, she took a swig. Everyone cheered, especially the drunk, who looked down at his tape recorder.

Veva was having a great time, as she sang her song. She finally felt that she was starting a good relationship with the press.

The next day several newspaper headlines featured:

VEVA CAROUSES WITH REPORTERS

VEVA SWIGS BOOZE

The front pages showed a picture of Veva swigging the bottle of rum.

Inside a radio studio, a disc jockey was speaking into his microphone.

"And now the hit of the week is your favorite Seattle first lady, Veva King singing her favorite song."

He pressed a button on a cart machine, which started a recording of Veva singing the song from the jet.

Inside a fancy ballroom, Charlie and Veva were dancing the night away. They were dressed very formally. It was a prestigious party.

Veva didn't seem too happy, though.

"I should have known better than to have trusted them."

She looked around to see that many of the other dancers were giving her glances of curiosity.

Charlie said, "Veva, you can't let them get you down."

She asked, "Doesn't it bother you that your wife is slowly but surely becoming the laughing stock of all Seattle?"

Charlie laughed, "Veva, you're new at this. The press does the same thing to all public people. They're just trying to sell more newspapers, get better ratings."

She replied, "I can't believe you're being so calm about this whole thing."

He looked her in the eye, "I understand how you feel, and if there was something I could do, I would, but, Veva, I'm a public person. Now you're a public person. It goes with the job, and there's nothing we can do about it. So, try and understand, okay?"

Veva was silent as they danced.

Charlie said, "These same people who are giving you a hard time, are the very ones who helped me get elected. Right now they're being a little strong on you, and I know it's hard on you. But, you knew being married to me wasn't always going to be a bowl of cherries, didn't you?"

Veva nodded, silently.

Charlie stopped dancing. He looked her in the eyes, real close, "come on, give me a smile, it can't be the end of the world. How 'bout it?"

Veva started smiling.

They hugged each other tightly.

Charlie grinned, "That's my girl."

Later that night in her bedroom, Veva's eye looked straight up to the ceiling. The room was fairly dark as Veva lay in the bed, staring. After a few moments of silence, she got up, walking over to her dresser. She turned on a radio.

She flipped from one station to another, from music to news shows, until she heard a woman talking, "I think she is a disgrace to this city, to her husband, and to the women of the world."

Veva sat at the edge of the bed.

The announcer said, "Thank you for your opinion. This is the Larry Paris show, where you can make your opinions be heard every morning from six to ten. This morning we are discussing the escapades of Seattle's first lady, Mrs. Veva King. If you have an opinion, just give us a call at 555-3752, and let your opinion be heard. The Larry Paris show, you're on the air."

Veva listened to a second of silence.

A man spoke, "I think she's a lousy singer."

The announcer replied, "Thank you for your opinion. This is the Larry Paris show, you're on the air."

Another woman spoke, "I agree with the lady that was on a few minutes ago. Veva King has a responsibility to the City of Seattle, to represent us in a dignified manner, and I don't think singing a stupid song to reporters while drinking a bottle of rum is dignified or right."

"Thank you for your opinion. This is the Larry Paris show, you're on the air . . ."

"I think she's trying to be honest, at least."

The announcer said, "Perhaps we are being unfair to Mrs. King. I doubt you are listening, Veva King, but if by any chance you are, why don't you give us a call and tell us your side of this intriguing story."

Veva immediately picked up the phone.

"Hello? This is Veva King and I would like to talk to Larry Paris. That's right."

~

The next day. Inside the radio studio. Larry Paris spoke into the microphone. Seated next to him was Veva, who was anxiously awaiting her cue.

Larry Paris said, "Good morning, opinion makers everywhere. This is the Larry Paris Show, where you can make your opinions be heard every morning from six to ten. This morning you are all in for a real treat. We have with us Mrs. Veva King, the wife of the Mayor. She's here in the flesh to answer your questions and to discuss whatever you want to discuss."

He glanced over to Veva who was quite nervous.

He continued, "Okay, we'll go to the phones to get our first question. Remember, if you have a question for the first lady of Seattle, now is your chance. Give us a call at 555-3752 and let your opinion be heard. The Larry Paris Show, you're on the air."

Veva listened to questions, answered them, laughed and smiled, noticeably enjoying herself.

"I learned a lot that day at the radio station. I learned that people are just people all over, and that most people are really nice and understanding. That day was the first time I ever had a chance to respond to all of the press I had been receiving ever since becoming Mrs. King, and I guess I got a lot off my chest."

The Family Life

Veva enjoyed playing with her three boys. They loved to ski, play Monopoly, ride horses, and be a normal family.

Charlie was always busy at work, making speeches, meeting world leaders, etc., but also he always tried to take time to have fun with the kids, wrestling playfully with the boys at every chance.

"The boys really grew up fast, but my first priority was to make sure that they led as normal a life as possible. Charlie was always busy on some important City problem, but he was always there when I or the kids needed him."

Inside the hospital room, Veva looked silently ahead. Barker had his pencil in his mouth.

"Well, Veva, we've been talking for a while now, and I think that it is a very interesting story. Young flower girl meets distinguished middle-aged politician, they date, fall in love, and marry. Except for a few runs in with the press and security people, it all seems like a fairy tale."

He looked at her curiously, continuing, "But there's

something missing. You've told me all about your superficial crisis, but that doesn't explain why you're here right now. Veva, I want you to trust me. You're no dummy. You know why you're here."

Veva looked up.

Doctor Barker said, "We've gone this far. Give me a chance to help you. Let's get into it, alright? Come on, let me go back with you to the last two years. So far life as you've told it has been not too bad, except for a few obstacles, but we all encounter obstacles."

Veva replied, "I am trying."

The doctor said, "I know you're trying. That's why I want to help you so much. Okay. Now something happened that changed this happy fairy tale. What was it?"

Veva looked ahead quietly.

The doctor started again, "Okay. So far you haven't mentioned any time spent with friends after your marriage to

Charlie. Didn't you have any friends?"

Veva looked up, "Sure, I had friends. Not that many, but a few. Alicia. She was a friend. I could talk to her."

"She <u>was</u> a friend? You're not friends any more?"

Veva seemed touchy on this subject, "Let me tell it my way, okay?"

The doctor grinded his teeth, "Okay, no problem."

Veva said, "Well, things were going pretty good for Charlie and I. He was busy with the affairs of the city and I was busy bringing up the boys. After I met Charlie I sort of lost touch with most of my friends from college, and most of the people I met as the Mayor's wife, well, were a lot older than I. That is, all except Alicia."

Veva was sitting on the floor of a bedroom with Alicia, a beautiful blonde Palestinian woman. She was very young and they were having a great time. It looked almost like a slumber party.

"I met her first in 1974 when a diplomat from the Middle East paid Charlie a friendship visit. He brought with him his beautiful wife, Alicia. The first time I met her I knew that we would be friends. We were just two girls, sitting and giggling in my bedroom, me in my jeans, she in her expensive fancy clothes."

The women giggled.

"I was six months pregnant and here I was dancing with famous celebrities. Movie stars, and princes from Europe.

I remember dancing with a future king. A real nice fellow, well, anyway, ha, ha, we're dancing at a great prestigious ball, and the maternity gown I had on had this real low cut top. Well, I catch him looking right at my breasts. You should have seen his face turn red. He looks at me and says, 'My father always told me to look people in they eyes'. Ha, ha."

They both broke up, laughing.

Alicia said, "I have met him. A very charming young man."

Veva replied, "Yes, he is. Have you met Castro?"

Alicia nodded, "He too is charming. Almost too charming."

Veva agreed, "I know what you mean. We visited Cuba last year, and he really knows how to talk to the ladies. You should have heard the story he told me. We were talking about something, I can't remember what it was, when he started to give me compliments."

Alicia said, "He is a very articulate speaker."

"At one point he was talking about eyes. He said that his eyes weren't very strong, and that every day he forces himself to stare at the sun to make them stronger. Then he really got me when he said he finds it hard. Then he asked me what he finds a lot harder. He said it was to look at the blue in my eyes."

Alicia said, "That's very nice."

Veva continued, "I know. A chill went right up my spine. And you know something, on the trip home Charlie asked me the craziest question."

"He was jealous of Castro?"

Veva laughed, "I couldn't believe it. Charlie told me he was afraid I was going to ask for asylum."

They giggled.

Veva said, "Alicia, I've only been the wife of the Mayor for a few years, now, and I guess, the hardest thing I've had to adjust to is this fish tank life. If it isn't the press, it's those funny looking apes in pin-striped suits."

Alicia said, "Security people. I know what you mean. Everything has been changed these last few years, with all the terrorists and the many assassinations attempts. We cannot help but be cautious."

"I try not to think about it," said Veva.

Alicia looked at her friend, "Your life isn't so bad, Veva. If you only knew how lucky you are. You husband will leave politics one day and then you'll be free. Mine is a life sentence."

Veva looked at her friend.

Alicia said, "Veva, it's not easy to find good friends, especially in our positions, but I can truly say that I am glad I can call you friend."

Veva was moved. They hugged.

"You know, one of these days we should rent a little house in London or New York, where we could escape from all the commotion on holidays."

Alicia agreed, "Yes, we could become, what do they call them, jet setters."

They laughed.

The TV News was on. Correspondent Frankie Shore

spoke, "Mayor King said today he is ready for the election.

Charlie was seen making the speech.

Shore continued, "Close sources to the Mayor confirm this reporter's opinion that this election should prove to be a tough one for the Charlie King."

Veva watched the program with Charlie in their living room.

Shore said, "King's problems seem to lie not in his programs, but in his own personal style. Many Seattle residents expect rousing rhetoric from their Mayor where King has consistently provided what many consider a too intellectual and arrogant"

Veva looked over to Charlie, who had a gloomy look on his face.

"Charlie, do you think it's that bad?"

"Oh, we'll win," he said, "but it's going to be tough."

Veva walked over to him, and sat on his lap, hugging.

"Charlie, I know how you've felt about me when it comes to your work, and all that, but I really think I could help you in this election."

Charlie said, "Now, Veva."

Veva jumped up, "Charlie! Look at any election in the world. The wives of the candidates can be a real asset to a campaign."

She looked at him sternly.

"Charlie, I'm not going to take no for an answer. Charlie, let me help you, please?"

Charlie was silent. After a few seconds of thought, he smiled.

"Okay, but nothing too crazy, okay?"

Veva smiled, "Alright!"

She hugged him tightly.

The campaign picked up speed. Veva could be seen speaking in front of women's clubs, colleges, and even girl scout troops.

Charlie made speech after speech after speech.

"Well, I really got into this new job. For the first time Charlie was letting me help him in his work, and I don't care if the press were assholes, and the days so long, I was finally doing something worthwhile."

Veva was working very hard to help Charlie on speeches, shaking hands, drinking at dinner parties. As the campaign continued Veva started getting irritable, tired, and finally exhausted.

The night of the election. Everyone was standing in front of TV screens.

Inside a back room, Charlie and Veva were seated, Charlie exuberantly happy, Veva exhausted.

"I did it, Veva. I won!"

"That's, uh, great, Charlie."

Charlie noticed her fatigue, "The people have spoken and now I can really make some changes."

He paced around the room, "Only a few men are blessed with such a responsibility. I hope I serve the people well."

Later that night, in the bedroom, Veva was lying on her bed talking into the phone.

"Alicia, it's good to hear from you."

Alicia said, "Veva! I am so happy for you, Charlie has won a great victory."

"I guess. I don't know, Alicia. I thought I would be ecstatic, but all I feel is anger."

"Anger? Who at? Charlie?"

"I know, I'm supposed to be happy and all that, but this was my first campaign, and I really worked hard! Probably harder than I've ever worked in my whole life. I thought Charlie would win and everything, but I think I really did some good. Talking to all those people, and shaking hands; it was truly an experience."

Veva got intense.

"But I can't believe it! Charlie didn't even thank me for helping him. I just cannot understand it. He's ungrateful."

Alicia said, "Veva, you've been through a lot these past weeks. Calm down. Charlie has probably just forgotten to thank you, he's under a lot of pressure and sometimes people forget."

Veva said, "You might be right, Alicia, but this is really making me mad. I don't think I'll ever forget or forgive this."

"Veva, talk to him. Get this anger you feel out into the open. You cannot let it build up inside. Talk to him, okay?"

"Thanks, Alicia. You're a good friend. Let me think about it for a while."

Veva put down the receiver.

The streets of Seattle. Veva walked through the crowds, looking in store windows, sitting on benches.

At the Seattle International Airport, Veva sat on a bench, watching the crowds go by.

A loudspeaker announced, "United Airlines Flight 774 to Paris, France, Now boarding at gate 45."

She looked up at the loudspeaker. She stood up and walked hurriedly toward an array of phone booths. She looked through her purse and found a coin.

"Let me speak to Charlie. Charlie? Yes, I know, I'm sorry. Charlie, I've been feeling a little stir crazy lately, and, well, I think I could use a vacation. I'm at the airport right now, and, I'm going to go to Paris for a few days to relax. Okay? No problem. I'll call you when I get there. Bye, bye. I love you."

She put the receiver down and rushed toward the ticket counter.

As the jetliner took off from the runway, inside the jet, Veva looked out the jet window, watching the clouds go by.

"I had taken a few short trips by myself before, but this was the first time that I had gone trying to escape."

She picked up her purse and flipped through it. She pulled out a wallet. In it were many pictures, of Charlie, her parents, her sisters, her children. Slowly she eyed each picture, carefully. From behind Charlie's picture she pulled out a wrinkled photo of Tony.

Veva smiled, reminiscing in her mind.

"It had been a long time, and I had no real right to be thinking of Tony, but I couldn't help myself."

She turned the picture over. On the back were the words, "NEW ADDRESS: 547 LE PIO LANE, ARIS, FRANCE"

Veva put the picture back behind Charlie's and into the purse. She aimed her eyes to the clouds outside her window.

"I told myself that I would just be visiting an old friend, that I wasn't doing anything wrong. For all Charlie knew, I was visiting the art galleries and museums."

The plane landed. Veva drove a car through the streets of Paris, looking for Tony's house.

She Veva walked up and rang the bell to his home. An old woman answered.

"Oui?"

Veva responded in French, "Can you tell me, does Tony Lewis live here?"

The woman said, "Tony Lewis?"

She had a blank look on her face.

Veva asked, "How long have you lived here?"
The woman answered, "Four years."
"Has someone called Tony Lewis left a forwarding address?"
The woman's face suddenly turned red and she started to tremble.
"I'm sorry. I'm sorry. I did not remember his name."
Veva said, "You know who I'm talking about?"
"I'm so sorry. Your friend Tony Lewis died, I heard from a gentleman down at the parlor. Tony Lewis. Nice man. Why did he do it? I cannot understand why these young people do such things."
Veva yelled, "What are you talking about? Where is Tony?"
"He committed suicide a few months back. I'm so sorry."

Veva began to tremble. Her face turned red. Her eyes got watery. She started to run away, almost getting hit by a taxi. The cab driver jumps out, yelling. Veva went to her car and in a moment of solitude, began to sob.

Inside the airplane, she looked straight ahead, then o over to the clouds.

The jet landed at the airport.

A limo rushed down the street. Veva just sat there, sullen and quiet.

Veva told the driver to stop the car. She got out.

She walked over to a bunch of hippies who were standing at a street corner.

The limo driver was confused. After a few moments Veva returned to the car. She has a strange smile on her face. She got back into the car.

Inside the limo, Veva looked down at her purse. In her hand were a handful of marijuana cigarettes.

The limo approached the Mayor's Mansion.

Inside the mansion, Veva quickly came through the front

door, with her driver not far behind.

The many maids and servants watched Veva as she rushed up the stairs.

Inside a bathroom, Veva turned on the lights, and locked the door. She pulled out one of the cigarettes. She fondled it as she looked at herself in the mirror.

After a few moments, she lit it. Her facial expression turned happy. The room became smoky and her smiles turned to laughter.

Charlie was reading a newspaper as he ate his dinner.

Veva sat quietly across the table, her eyes squinting as if she is slightly stoned. She smiled.

"Well, dear, how was your day?" she asked.

Charlie didn't look up from his paper.

"Oh, fine, dear."

Veva did not like to be ignored.

"The boys and I had a fun day, riding horses after school."

Charlie continued to look at his paper.

"That's fine, dear," he replied.

Veva said, "Stevie fell and hurt his leg, but luckily it was only a scratch."

"Uh, yes, that's fine, dear," Charlie replied. He wasn't paying any attention to what she was saying.

Veva had flames in her eyes, now. She looked at Charlie, who seems to be hiding behind the newspaper. She looked around and picked up her salad bowl. She smiled as she nonchalantly poured it onto her own head. Then she just sat there waiting to see if Charlie noticed her.

A maid walked into the room. When she saw Veva all covered with salad, she stopped in her tracks.

"Oh, my Lord!"

Charlie turned to her and then looked over to Veva.

He yelled, "What the hell."

He stood up, "Veva! What the hell is going on here!"

She laughed, "I just wanted to see if you were listening to anything I was saying."

"Veva, I don't know what games you're playing, but I'm not in any mood for them."

She yelled back, "Games? Is that what this all is?"

"Veva! Stop it," he screamed.

The maid helped clean Veva's head. Veva looked embarrassed. Charlie walked out of the room and into his study. After a few moments, Veva went to him.

Veva entered the room. Charlie was sitting in a recliner, reading a book. Veva approached him.

"Charlie, I'm sorry."

"What was all that about?"

"I don't know. I've been a little edgy lately, I'm sorry. It's probably from the campaign and all that."

Charlie put his arm around her.

"It has been a bit hectic around here lately, hasn't it? Veva, why don't you take a vacation—why not go up and see your mother for a couple of weeks? The kids are in school and their nannies and I should be able to handle them okay, what do you say?"

Veva relaxed and smiled as they hugged.

"Thanks, Charlie. I think it might do me some good."

"Okay, then do it, but Veva, I don't want anything like what just happened to ever happen again. I won't condone it."

"I'm sorry."

They hugged.

At the airport, Veva waited in anger at the ticket counter. She was eager for a good vacation with her family.

When she made it to the front of the line, she noticed a crowd building up around a television set. She looked over to the counter person.

Veva said, "Say, what's going on over there?"

She pointed over to the crowd.

"Oh, something about a helicopter crash in the Middle East."

"Huh?"

She got her ticket and walked over to the set.

TV reporter said, "The helicopter crashed in a sudden rainstorm instantly killing all those aboard. Among the passengers was the Queen of Jordan, the beautiful wife of King Hussein, Queen Alicia."

Veva was stunned.

"She was on a return flight after supposedly visiting a local village hospital. Today the world mourns the death of a beautiful and benevolent person, Queen Alicia, Queen of Jordan."

Tears ran down Veva's face. A gentlemen saw her and approached her.

"Is everything okay, lady?"

Veva pushed him away, "Leave me alone."

She rushed over to a phone booth. She dialed a number.

"Hello? This is Mrs. King, yes, is Mr. King there? Let me speak with him. What? I don't care who he's talking to, let me speak with him. Tell him it's important."

She waited a few moments.

"What! He's too busy to talk? Okay, tell him I'll talk to him later!"

She slammed down the receiver.

"Jesus! Son of a bitch!"

Her eyes got real watery. She tried to wipe them. She went into the bathroom and into a stall. She wiped her eyes with a handkerchief. She looked through her purse until she found what she's looking for—a marijuana cigarette. She looked around and lit it. After a few moments, she started to relax, and then broke down and cried her heart out.

Later in an airplane, Veva sat by a window. She was sitting amongst a bunch of young men. She laughed, noticeably stoned. In front of her sat several little liquor bottles.

Talking like a narrator to the Doctor, Veva said, "Somehow, I don't know how or at least I can't remember how, I ended up in New York at a big party. Charlie didn't know where I was, and to be honest, I didn't really care."

At the party, Veva laughed wildly, surrounded by several middle-aged men, who were wearing tuxedos.

"Mrs. King . . ."

"Call me Veva, Senator."

"Okay, Veva, what do you Seattle people think about our Yankees?"

They laughed.

Veva said, "Well, Senator, us Seattle people do not like the Yankees."

Veva was pretty well drunk by now. Out of the corner of her eye, she could see a tall, dark, and handsome man who was constantly giving her the eye. Veva seemed curious about him. She looked right at him, him at her. Slowly he walked over to her.

Pendleton said, "Mrs. King."

Veva replied, "I don't believe I've had the honor."

He said, "I beg your pardon. My name is John Pendleton, my friends call me Jake."

"Nice to meet you, Jake."

They looked each other right in the eyes. A band from the other side of the room started to play a song.

Pendleton said, "Would you like to dance, Mrs. King."

Veva smiled, "Please call me Veva, Mr. Pendelton."

"Veva, I would be honored to share this dance with such a beautiful woman."

Veva smiled as Pendleton held his hand out for her.

"Why thank you, Mr. Pendleton."

"Call me Jake."

He smiled as he led her out to the dance floor. They created strange looks from almost everybody on the dance floor.

Veva and Pendleton danced very close together, and for most of the night. Veva seemed very much moved by this handsome man from the South.

Later that night, they made passionate love.

The next morning, Pendleton was asleep in bed. He awakened at the unique sound of a person vomiting. He got up out of the bed, wrapping a sheet around him as he went toward the noise. He looked into the bathroom where Veva was puking her guts out.

Veva looked up to him. She started crying heavily.

The King bedroom was pitch black. Charlie was awakened by some strange noises. He was sound asleep. He got up, put on his robe, and headed down the stairs.

Charlie scratched his head in wonderment as to where the sounds were coming from. He heard glass breaking.

Charlie opened the kitchen door to find Veva silhouetted in the darkness by light from the open refrigerator. He turned on the kitchen light.

"Veva! What the hell's going on here? When did you get in?"

She looked terrible. Her eyes were bloodshot. Next to her on the counter was an empty Vodka bottle.

Charlie saw the bottle and became enraged.

He walked up to her, grabbed her, and slapped her in the face.

"Have you been unfaithful to me?" he asked.

Veva did not say anything.

"Have you? Have you?"

Veva started sobbing. Charlie looked at her for a moment and then turned around and slowly, step by step, went up the stairs.

Veva wanted to follow him, but she did not.

As Charlie made it to the top up the stairs, two of the children were seen at the top, rubbing their eyes to get the sleepiness out.

Stevie said, "Mommy? Daddy, is mommy home?"

Michael said, "Mommy!"

Charlie picked them both up into his arms.

"Let's go back to bed, boys. Mommy will see you in the morning."

He looked down the stairs from the top and then closed the door behind him as he entered his bedroom.

Veva fell to her knees in the kitchen, crying. She looked over to the counter and saw a couple large knives.

~~~

The next morning, Veva awoke to a ray of morning sunshine. The bright light beamed through the kitchen window.

She was laying on the floor, the empty Vodka bottle next to her, and a large knife in her hands. She looked at the knife and then held her pounding head.

"I've felt this headache before."

She lifted herself off the floor, tightening her grip on the knife. She walked to the living room where several large pictures of Charlie, her, and their children hung on the walls. Veva stared at the pictures for a moment, picking up the family portrait and looking at it closely.

She looked up. She was a little startled when she saw her reflection in a large wall mirror. She walked up to the mirror, staring at her own eyes.
~~~

The lawn of the Mayor's mansion was green and huge.

It was snowing that day. In the distance a woman could be seen running.

It was Veva.

She ran through the snow, barefoot, and with the knife in one hand.

She stopped in the middle of a field, falling to her knees.

Her boys screamed, "Mommy!"

They ran up to her, crying loudly.

Veva looked at them, but then pushed them away as they tried desperately to hug her.

The boys were startled that their mother pushed them away.

Charlie ran up. He grabbed the boys, who were hysterically crying. He put them down for a second, walked over to Veva, taking the knife from her hand. He handed her shoes.

Veva was silent. When Charlie pulled the knife from

her. She started crying, holding herself.

The boys yelled, "MOMMY!"

Charlie became angry. He yelled, "Veva!"

Veva stood still. She looked up to him, slowly getting up. Then she began walking down the road.

The boys cried.

Stevie asked, "Daddy, why is mommy doing this?"

Charlie shook his head, "I don't know, son."

Veva walked slowly through the snow. She walked down the road.

Inside the hospital room, Barker and Veva sat quietly. Veva had her head down. She looked up to show watery eyes and streaks of mascara running down her face.

"And, well, here we are," she said.

Barker silently looked at her.

"Do you love this Pendleton fellow?"

Veva said, "Shit, I don't know."

"You've been through a lot."

"Doctor, I've sat here and told you my whole story. Is that all you have to say? That I've been through a lot?"

The doctor said, "What do you want me to say?"

Veva said, "I don't know. Tell me what my problem is. Tell me what to do."

"I can't tell you what to do. You tell me! What is your problem?"

Veva was silent for a time. Then she said, "I feel like I'm Alice in Wonderland. Everyone is watching me. I must be paranoid or something."

The doctor replied, "Veva, everyone <u>is</u> watching you. That's not paranoia, it's reality."

"But, doctor, I feel hostile. I have illusions of grandeur. I think I am somebody."

"You <u>are</u> somebody! Veva, I want you to stay here for a couple more days, to think things out. Think about what you've told me, and what it all means. Veva, when it comes down to it, you've got to make your own decisions. I'll be around. You take some time and pretty soon it will all come together. When it does, you tell a nurse to get me. Okay?"

Veva sat there silently. Barker watched her for a moment and then he left the room.

She gazed to the ceiling. She laid on her back, her eyes began to close.

She could see her whole life story dissolve past her. Images of Charlie and Tony from Tahiti; her kissing Tony in his apartment; her and Charlie at the Lake; Charlie crying after his friend's murder; the slumber party with Alicia; her and Charlie laughing, kissing, and embracing; Pendleton at the party; the Moroccan orgy; and finally the images of the faces of her three children crying for their mother. The images flew faster and faster in her mind, until suddenly everything went black.

The next morning, the room was brighter. Veva was asleep.

Everything was fuzzy. Slowly she focused in to a middle aged man who looked over her. As the focus became sharper, she recognized him as a priest.

The priest said, "Good morning, Mrs. King."

She sat up.

The priest asked, "Whatever are you doing here, Mrs. King?"

Veva opened her eyes wider.

"You should be at home with your children!"

Veva stared silently.

Outside the hospital, it was mass confusion as numerous

TV and radio news crews had assembled.

Frankie Shore, the TV reporter, was getting ready to speak to the camera, his hand holding his ear.

"This is Frankie Shore on location at the front steps of Seattle General Hospital where Veva Carter King, wife of the Seattle Mayor, is about to be released after 28 days of medical observation. There seems to be a cloak of mystery as doctors and hospital officials have agreed not to release Mrs. King's reason for the hospitalization. Speculation has it that Mrs. King has been here convalescing an alleged abortion. Well, here she comes now.

The crowd roared with excitement. Reporters screamed as they are held back by numerous policemen.

Veva, Charlie, Doctor Barker, and the King children came out of the hospital entrance.

Veva's eyes were bloodshot from crying. They all walked together, Veva holding Charlie's hand.

A reporter screamed, "Mrs. King, how about a statement?"

Another journalist yelled, "Is it true you had an abortion?"

Several other reporters yelled questions to Veva and Charlie.

A valet of Charlie's walked up to the podium set up by the press for questions.

"The Mayor and his wife have no statement to make at this time, thank you."

The valet walked away. The reporters let out yells of anger.

Veva looked to the press men and women. She stopped Charlie and the others.

"Wait."

The crowd instantly turned silent as she approached the podium. She looked around to the crowd.

She saw the faces of the crowd. Men and women of all

ages. They seemed sincere and earnest as they waited for Veva's voice.

Veva looked back to Charlie. Charlie stared to the ground. The three children had tears rolling down their cheeks.

Dr. Barker smiled, hoping to give her encouragement. Veva glanced back to the crowd, a tear rolling down her face.

"I told myself that I wasn't going to say anything today. But I just cannot help it. Why don't you leave me alone? Can't you feel any compassion for me? I don't know how long I have been here, but I, uh, I am suffering from severe emotional stress."

Her voice cracked.

She continued, "Please go away and leave me alone! Please!"

Slowly she walked back with the others and headed for the car. Charlie gave her a big hug.

The crowd was stunned.

~

The King family jumped into the limo. Doctor Barker closed the door behind them. Veva looked out the back window of the car. She could see Dr. Barker get smaller in the distance as the car pulled away.

Charlie looked to her and to his children. Doctor Barker watched the car pull away.

~

The reporters waited and waited. Finally the Mayor's press secretary appeared at the podium.

"The Mayor has the following statement.

"Charlie and Veva King announce that based on Mrs. King's wishes, they shall be living separate and apart.

Mrs. King relinquishes all privileges as wife of the mayor and wishes to leave the marriage and pursue an independent career. The Mayor will have custody of their sons, giving Veva generous access to them. The mayor accepts Veva King's decision with regret and both pray that their separation will lead to a better relationship between themselves."

"Grounded"

It was a typical American suburban neighborhood. The kids were playing basketball in a driveway.

Jimmy said, "That's the way, Mikey."

Mikey made a pass and Jimmy made the shot.

"Awesome shot," Mikey said.

The other kids shrugged.

Dennis, the bully, yelled, "Foul, the shot doesn't count."

"Foul?" said Mikey. "There was no foul!"

Dennis replied, "What do you want to do about it? I called a foul."

"No problem, Dennis," said Jimmy. "Mikey let him shoot."

Mikey threw the ball to Dennis reluctantly.

Dennis said, "Mikey, you have to learn to follow the rules."

"Just shoot."

Dennis missed the shot.

Mikey laughed big time, "Cheaters never prosper."

"Who are you calling a cheater?"

"Just play the game, guys," yelled Jimmy.

Dennis bounced the ball off his foot and it started rolling.

The basketball rolled. Slowly, very slowly it rolled up the driveway. Jimmy and Mikey silently looked at each other.

The ball skipped across the pavement of the street.

Jimmy yelled, "Oh, no, get the ball!"

Dennis looked scared.

Mikey said, "I'll get it." Mikey chased the ball.

In almost slow motion, the ball headed for the house across the street.

Jimmy yelled, "Hurry, Mikey."

Dennis screamed, "Quick, before it reaches the Templeton house."

Mikey grabbed the ball, looking up at the house.

The house looked ominous. It had weeds everywhere and looked like it was a big beautiful house forty years ago. Now it was a scary place.

Suddenly a cat jumped out of the bushes.

Mikey screamed at the top of his lungs. He was frozen with fear.

Jimmy yelled, "Mikey." Jimmy ran over, picked up Mikey with the ball, carrying them back to the safety of Jimmy's home driveway. Mikey was still screaming.

"It's all okay, Mikey. You are safe."

Jimmy looked back over to the Templeton house.

"That sure is a scary place."

Mikey said, "I heard that vampires used to live there."

Jimmy replied, "Sometimes I hear scary noises at night."

The kids continued their hoops like nothing happened. They bounced the basketball and were thankful they were at the safe haven across the street.

A sedan drove up to the scary house across the street.

The kids stopped their basketball game. All they could see were the mirror sunglasses.

Dill, a husky, tanned man in a suit was in the driver's seat.

The basketball bounced in slow motion. Jimmy looked over to the strange men.

Dill looked over to Lenny, a pale-faced, skinny guy.

They got out of the car, and walked slowly up to the house.

The kids stared at the strangers. The men approached the front door to the home.

Lenny said, "Looks like a nice neighborhood."

Dill didn't say much. Lenny pulled off his sunglasses. He looked over to the kids playing basketball.

Down the street, housewives watched the men from their kitchen windows.

Dill said, "Let's get inside right now."

The kids watched the men. Mikey was getting scared.

"I've gotta go," said Mikey. He ran down the street.

Jimmy yelled, "Mikey, where are you going?" Mikey was long gone down the street.

Mikey yelled back, "I'll call you later, Jimmy."

Dennis said, "Maybe they are a couple of fags."

Jimmy said, "No, they are probably brothers, or maybe they are FBI agents on the lookout for drug dealers."

Inside the house across the street, Dill opened up his briefcase.

"I really think this whole thing sucks," he said.

Dill pulled out a weird gizmo from the briefcase.

"Your kind of people belong where we had you, behind bars."

Lenny looked closely at the gizmo.

Dill said, "Just because of overcrowding they are going to

let you live like you are in a country club."

He checked the batteries on the gizmo.

"Well, this device will make sure you are a good boy."

He pressed some buttons on the gizmo.

"Let me have your arm. Are you right or left handed?"

Lenny answered, "Right."

Dill said, "Give me your right arm."

He grabbed Lenny's arm roughly, handcuffing the electronic gizmo around the arm like a large bracelet.

Lenny yelled, "Ow! It's too tight."

Dill laughed, "I like it better tight."

Lenny said, "It really hurts."

"You'll get used to it," said Dill.

Lenny tried to loosen the gizmo from his arm.

Dill said, "Here are the rules. If you make any mistakes on these rules you will be back in the slammer faster than you can say Sorry Charlie."

Lenny didn't appreciate Dill's humor.

Dill continued, "This electronic device has been assigned to you for the next 180 days. You must not attempt to tamper with the device. If you do you will be placed back in the slammer. If you attempt to leave this house the device will shock you and automatically radio your location to me and I will personally put you back in the slammer. If you attempt to tamper with the batteries on this device you will be subject to electric shock and automatically sent back to the slammer."

Dill pressed a button on the gizmo. The machine started making a loud screeching noise.

Across the street, the kids could hear the screeching noise.

Jimmy said, "Hey, Listen to that noise."

Dennis said, "Sounds like a dead ghost."
Jimmy replied, "All ghosts are dead, stupid."
Back in the house across the street, Lenny was holding his ears. He could not stand the loud noise.
Dill sneered a sick smile as he deactivated the gismo, causing the noise to stop.
Lenny said, "Yes, sir, of course, sir, I understand the rules of my parole, sir."

Dill touched the machine with a pen and a giant electrical shock could be seen and heard.
Dill said, "Five thousand volts. Knock the dickens out of a fellow."
He laughed, "Well I better go now."
Lenny looked at him.
Dill said, "Oh, I almost forgot."
He handed Lenny a plain white envelope.
"From a friend."

The kids watched as Dill exited the house across the street.

Jimmy said, "Here they come."

They faked like they were just playing basketball.

Dill walked over to the kids.

Jimmy said, "Hello, sir."

Dill answered, "Look, kids, I have to talk with you."

Down the street, a couple of housewives named Millie and Joanie looked through the kitchen window, watching all this.

Joannie said, "I wonder what is going on over at the Templeton house?"

Millie said, "Looks like new neighbors."

Dill pulled out a badge.

"Listen kids."

Dennis remarked, "Wow, a real badge."

Dill said, "that's right, a real badge. Now this is an order from the police."

The kids were impressed.

"You see that house across the street?" Dill pointed at Lenny's house. "Due to a top-secret situation, you are hereby ordered to stay at least 100 feet from that house."

Jimmy said, "No way."

Dill asked, "You don't want to get arrested, do you?"

The kids said "No."

Dill said, "Then shut up and follow orders."

The kids stood at attention.

Dill sternly said, "Here's my card. If you see the gentleman I arrived with attempt to leave that house, I want you to immediately call me at the number on this card."

He handed the card to Jimmy.

Dill looked Jimmy in the eye, "Do you understand?"

Jimmy looked at the card.

Dill repeated, "Do you understand?"

"Yes, sir," Jimmy said, "I think."

Dill said, "Remember, stay at least 100 feet away from that house."

Dill jumped in his car and pulled away.

Inside the house, Lenny watched from the window. He opened the envelope Dill gave him.

Inside the envelope, he found a credit card and a note. It was from his mother. The phone began to ring. He slowly picked up the receiver.

It was Dill. "Just wanted you to know that I am watching you. If you try to escape or do anything weird I will personally smash your skull."

Lenny asked, "What's with the credit card?"

Dill said, "I know nothing about any credit card." He smiled.

Inside Millie's house, the housewives agreed to make a cake for the new neighbors.

The kids looked over at the Templeton house.

Jimmy said, "we need to find out what's going on in that house."

Lenny watched the kids from his window. He picked up the phone.

"Hi, Ma, it's Lenny." There was silence at the other end of the call.

"Come on, Ma. Talk to me. How many times do I have to say I am sorry?"

The silence continued.

"Well, Ma, I am settled in the new house. I can't leave, but you can visit if you want to."

More silence.

"Okay, Ma. I know you are listening. I wanted to thank you for the credit card and the note."

Still silent.

"Well, gotta go now, Ma. Lot's of things for me to do. Hope you can come see me, Ma. Well, bye, Ma."

A tear formed in his eye.

Over at Jimmy's house, the family sat around the table eating dinner. Jimmy looked around the table to Jimmy's Dad, Jimmy's Mom, and Wendy his little sister.

Over at Lenny's house, Lenny looked through the home. He pulled open drawers and opened every closet. He finally found a telephone book on the upper shelf in the hall closet.

Lenny flipped through the yellow pages until he came to the Ps.

"Pizza," he said.

He grabbed the phone, pointing at a big advertisement in the yellow pages for Pizza Delivery.

"Pepperoni Pizza, and a big bottle of soda." He pulled out his mother's credit card. "Yeah, let's put it on a credit card."

Over at Jimmy's house, Jimmy was in his room, doing his homework on his personal computer. His sister walked in.

"Hi Jimmy. What do you know about the new neighbor?"

"Wendy, why do you ask?"

"I think he looks cute."

Over at Lenny's house, Lenny ate with his mouth open. The pizza tasted so good. He looked through the yellow pages until he finds the page called "escort services". He called the number.

"Do you deliver?"

Over at Jimmy's house, Jimmy scanned the internet on his computer. He found some old newspaper clippings.

He punched in the words "templeton" and "house" and started a search. Several graphic articles popped up.

"Multiple Murder"

"Suicide."

"Devil Worship"

Jimmy discovered each of these stories was talking about the mystery house across the street.

He discovered that many mysterious things had happened over the years including a murder, a suicide, and other sick things.

He learned that in the 1800's it was the sight of a slaughterhouse.

Over at Lenny's house, Lenny talked with the hooker. They had sex.

Over at Jimmy's house, Jimmy's dad knocked on the door.

"I hear that you had a run in with a cop."

Jimmy said, "I did not have a run in, just a discussion."

Jimmy's dad warned him, "Jimmy, you cannot do anything to jeopardize your scholarship to that big college back east." Jimmy said, "I won't dad."

Over at Lenny's house, Dill knocked on the door. He wanted to surprise Lenny. Just as he entered the front door, the hooker exited out the back window.

Over at Millie's house, Millie watched the hooker leave out the back door.

Over at Lenny's house, Dill checked the gizmo on Lenny's arm. The door bell rang.

Dill went to the door.

It was the neighbors, Millie and Joanie.

"Hi, we are Millie and Joanie, your neighbors."

Dill looked over to Lenny.

Millie continued, "We want to give you, our new neighbors, a nice homemade pie."

They handed Dill a big beautiful pie.

Millie noticed the gizmo on Lenny's arm. Lenny noticed that Millie noticed the gizmo.

Dill said, "Why that is certainly very neighborly, isn't it Lenny?" He looked over to Lenny.

"Thank you, ladies."

After the women left, Dill punched Lenny in the stomach.

"Why did you do that?" yelled Lenny.

"You should respect those ladies. They did not have to bring you a pie. They did not have to be so neighborly."

Lenny nodded, "you are right, Dill. Lenny looked closely at Dill.

"Dill, who are you really working for? And don't tell me it's only the cops."

Dill squinted his eyes, "What do you mean, Lenny?"

Lenny said, "you are working for her, aren't you?"

"I don't know what you are talking about."

Lenny leaned over, "You are working on the side for my Mom, aren't you?"

The next day, over at Jimmy's tree fort, the kids gathered in a circle.

One of the kids asked, "what are we going to do about the house across the street?"

Jimmy said, "let's start taking turns doing surveillance."

"Great idea, Jimmy!"

The kids cheered as they gave each other high fives.

Over at Lenny's house, Lenny watched as a big screen TV was being delivered. He looked around at the house now. It was filled with lots of expensive furniture.

Over at Jimmy's tree fort, the kids watched the action.

"Look at that expensive big screen."

"I can't believe all the gadgets that guy has."

"He's got the best video game system I ever saw."

"He must be rich."

"Maybe he is a rock star or a famous writer who is renting the house so he can write his music or his new blockbuster movie?"

Over at Millie's house, Millie and Wendy talked about the stranger across the street.

Millie said, "Did you see that suspicious looking electronic gizmo on that man's arm?"

Over at Jimmy's tree fort, the kids decided to try some new tactics to learn more about the stranger.

"Let's go knock on the strangers door acting as if we were doing a survey for a school project?"

"Yeah," the kids yelled.

Over at Lenny's house the kids knocked on the door.

"Hello, sir, we are doing a class project, a survey of people moving into the area. Sort of a census."

Lenny smiled, "Sure, come on in."

Over at Millie's house, Millie watched from her window.

"Oh, no, don't go in there."

Over at Lennie's house the kids were in awe with the big screen and the expensive furniture and stereos.

Jimmy asked, "Sir, could you answer a few questions for our survey?"

"Sure, go ahead, kid, as long as you don't get too personal," Lenny said.

"Where are you from, sir?"

"That's personal."

"Oh," said Jimmy. "How long are you planning to stay, sir?"

"That's personal."

"Oh," said Jimmy. "What is that strange machine on your arm, sir?"

Lenny smiled, "Oh, that is a specialized medical gadget."

"What for?"

"It is for a special medical experiment." Lenny laughed.

"Oh," said Jimmy.

"Thanks, kids for thinking about me for this survey, but I think it's about that time."

"Thank you sir for your help with our survey."

And with that, the kids left.

Back at Jimmy's fort, the kids got into a huddle.

"I don't trust him," said Jimmy.

"I don't believe a word he says," said Billy.

Jimmy said, "I think this requires a major, full blown investigation."

"Yeah!" the boys screamed.

Jimmy delegated different jobs to each of the kids.

Over at Lennie's house, Lenny sat in a big easy chair, listening to classical music. He tried to open up the band on the gizmo on his arm.

Over at the County Courthouse, Jimmy and the kids climbed the giant stairs to the entrance.

A security guard stopped them at the door.

"How can I help you gentlemen?" the security guard said.

Jimmy answered, "We want to do some research for a school project."

"What kind of research are you looking for?" said the guard.

"We would like to research if a guy has a record."

"A record?"

"Yes," Jimmy said. "A crime record, a prison record, a bad guy record."

"Yeah," said another kid. "We want to find out if a guy is bad."

"Oh, that kind of record," said the security guard. "You can go to the Records Department on the Sixth floor."

"Thanks," yelled the kids.

"But," said the guard, "you need to go through the metal detector."

"No problem, sir," said the kids. One by one they went through the big detector. They ran over and got to the elevator.

The security guard picked up a telephone.

"Get me Detective Broome."

~

Over at Lennie's house, Lenny was feeling lonely. He looked at his face in the reflection of a beer mug.

"I was framed," he told himself.

He was sad.

"She told me she was nineteen years old and I believed her."

He started to watch an erotic movie on cable television.

"This is going to give me flashbacks."

Over at Jimmy's house, Jimmy's dad was giving his son a serious talk.

"Jimmy, all this mystery house stuff and this stranger stuff is hurting your grades."

"Yes, sir," said Jimmy.

"You need to start spending more time on your studies."

"Yes, sir," he said.

Dad stormed off up to his bedroom. Jimmy's mom gave Jimmy a big hug.

"I remember when the minute and moment you were born."

Jimmy looked up at his mother.

"Yes, Jimmy, you were the most beautiful thing I ever saw. I know that you mean well, and you have a natural curiosity about things."

"But Mom."

"But Jimmy, sometimes you need to know that there is a time and place for things. Right now the time is right for you to focus on your friends and your homework and playing ball, having fun."

"Yes, Mother."

"Jimmy, you have your whole life to be serious. Now you should just have fun being a kid, while you can."

"Yes, Mom."

~~~

The next day, one of the kids, Billy, decided he needed to know more about that house. So he went to the library.

He went to the desk with the sign "Information."

Billy asked the cute librarian, "How can I find out who owns a house?"

The librarian said, "well, there are a couple of ways to do it. You could go to a reverse directory."

"Reverse directory?" Billy said.

"It is a book that shows you the names of the owners of homes or businesses by street address."

"Do you have a reverse directory here?"

"Well, in fact we do. Follow me."
~~~

She led him over to a wall of big reference books. Billy watched her pull out a big red book.

"Here you go."

"Thank you, Madam."

He sat down at a large table. He pulled out a piece of paper from his pocket. It said, "271 Chapel Lane." He started turning the pages until he came to the letter C. His finger went down the page 100, 105.

"There it is." His finger pointed at 271. His finger went from 217 to the name.

"United States Department of Justice."

Billy wrote down on his paper the words. "United States Department of Justice."

"Uh, oh," he said.

Billy climbed up the tree to the fort. Inside he could tell there was a full house today.

"Hey Billy."

"Hey, guys," Billy said. "I've got some interesting news."

He told the kids, "the house is owned." He pulled out the white piece of paper and read, "United States Department of Justice."

The kids became silent.

"The government?"

"Yes."

"The government owns the house?"

"Yes, the librarian helped me look it up."

The kids started to speculate now.

"That guy must be an undercover cop."

"He could be a witness for the government on the witness protection program."

"Maybe he is a spy."

"Or maybe he is a prisoner on house arrest."

"He could be on quarantine for some strange disease."

Jimmy finally said, "bottom line is this guy is most likely a bad guy or a cop."

The car was in a hurry. Dill pulled over a block away from the house. He saw a newspaper boy on a bike.

"Hey, kid."

"Yes, sir?"

"Do you have a paper for that house number 217?"

"Yes, sir, I get paid extra for putting it on the porch."

Dill smiled. He pulled out a twenty dollar bill.

"Here is twenty dollars if you just put it on the driveway."

"I don't understand, sir. You want to pay me twenty dollars not to put it on the porch?"

"That's right, son."

"Ok, sure thing, mister."

Lenny looked out the window. He could see the newspaper boy riding up on his bike. The kid threw the newspaper on the driveway.

Lenny looked at the newspaper in his driveway. He did not know what to do. He looked at the gizmo on his arm.

Does he go get the newspaper and risk the gizmo going off or does he just sit there and not take a chance?

"You have to confront your fears," he told himself.

He slowly grabbed the doorknob. He timidly put one foot out, then another. Every second his eyes darted back and forth from the gismo to the newspaper, from the newspaper to the gismo.

Suddenly a hand picked up the newspaper. Lenny looked up and realized it was Dill. Quickly Lenny stepped back towards the house. He looked to Dill.

"Just trying to get the newspaper." Lenny said.

"You almost got fried for a newspaper," grinned Dill.

Dill looked over to across the street. The kids were watching his every move.

The kids waved at him.

Dill looked over to Lenny. "Lenny, have you been a bad boy?"

"They just knocked on my door doing a survey," Lenny said.

Dill angrily pushed Lenny back into the house with the newspaper and said "go back inside and shut the door".

The kids could see Dill walking their way. They scattered in all directions, except Jimmy. He just stood there waiting for Dill.

"Hello, sir," Jimmy said.

Dill yelled, "What the hell are you doing?"

"Shooting some hoops, sir."

Dill said, "I thought I told you to stay away from the house across the street."

"It's a free country, sir."

Dill said, "You think you are a wise guy, eh?"

"No, sir," Jimmy replied. "Just shooting some hoops on

my own personal property which by the way you are currently considered a trespasser."

From down the street, Jimmy could hear a voice. "Jimmy!"

It was Millie the neighbor lady.

"You, hoo, Jimmy. Jimmy Johnson. Who is your new friend?"

Dill looked over and saw the old lady Millie standing on her porch, shooting them with her camcorder. He smiled and waved.

"Just a family friend."

Jimmy yelled, "He's just leaving, Millie."

"Sorry I couldn't stay a little longer," said Dill.

Jimmy smiled, "Maybe another time."

Dill had a mean stare at Jimmy, "You can count on it. For your own good, son, stay away from the house and the man in that house across the street."

Jimmy asked, "What has he done? We know the house is owned by the government. Who is he? What did he do? Is he a criminal or a cop? Is he a good guy or a bad guy?"

Dill said, "I wish I could tell you. But I can't." Dill stomped away. He went over to Lenny's house, entering through the front door.

Dill yelled at Lenny, "You son of a bitch."

He called his superior.

"Yes, sir. He has made contact with some children in the neighborhood."

He yelled into the phone, "we must move him away from this type of environment, sir."

Getting red in the face, Dill slammed down the phone. He grabbed Lenny and a kitchen knife.

"I should cut off your ear, you asshole."

Dill crushed Lenny down to the floor. "Or better yet, how about I cut off your testicles?"

Lenny tried to push him away, but Dill was strong.

"In a lot of third world countries cutting the balls of molesters is common."

Dill pointed the knife at Lenny's private parts.

Lenny screamed, "I am not a molester."

Dill laughed, "yeah you are innocent. Haven't I heard that one before."

"I was framed by a 13 year-old girl who had a crush on me."

Dill pulled back, letting Lenny go. He looked around at the big screen TV and expensive furniture.

"This whole thing makes me sick. You make me sick." Dill slammed the door as he left.

Jimmy looked up at the ceiling in his bedroom. He was supposed to be sleeping, but he couldn't stop thinking.

His dad walked in.

"I heard that you were being a smart aleck with a police officer."

Jimmy said, "he isn't a police officer."

His Dad did not listen. He replied, "You are grounded, Jimmy."

"That's not fair," yelled Jimmy.

Down the hallway lay Wendy in her bed. She listened to all the yelling. She put her hands over her ears.

The kids were piled into Billy's oldest brother Bobby's car. Bobby had just gotten his drivers license. He wasn't supposed to be driving so many kids, but he was.

"Quiet, please," said Bobby. "I am trying to focus on my driving, please."

The kids quieted down.

"There he is," yelled one of the kids. He was pointing at the black car. It was Dill's car. He was driving.

"Follow that car," the kids yelled in harmony.

"Quiet, he might hear us," Billy said.

They quietly followed Dill in his car.

Over at Lenny's house, Lenny played chess on his computer. The doorbell rang.

He opened the door to see Wendy.

"Yes, can I help you?" Lenny asked.

Wendy screamed, "ever since you came into our neighborhood, everyone is yelling."

Lenny did not know what to say.

"I am sorry," he said.

He then broke down crying.

Wendy followed him into the house.

Over at Millie's house, Millie's head could be seen watching everything from her window. She saw Wendy going into Lenny's home.

Back at Lenny's house, Wendy and Lenny played chess.

"You play chess pretty well," said Lenny.

"My dad taught me," she answered.

"Your dad must be a smart guy," Lenny said.

"Yes, he is super smart."

Wendy looked over to the gizmo on Lenny's arm. "What is that thing?" she asked.

"Well, it is a present from a friend."

"What does it do?"

"It keeps track of where I am."

"What do you mean?"

"It has some kind of radio in it that is picked up by some satellite somewhere and it tells someone somewhere where I am at all times."

"You mean you are grounded?"

"Sort of, yeah, grounded."

~~~

Then Lenny did something bold, something he never should have done. He told her his whole life story.

~~~

The kids followed Dill. He pulled up to a big white building.

Billy and Mikey got out of the car and followed Dill into the building.

They followed him up some stairs.

Dill went through a door on the sixth floor. The kids were almost out of breath when they got to the door.

They slowly opened the door. They could see a hallway. They quietly walked down the hallway, looking at the names and numbers on the doors.

They realized that they were in some kind of law

enforcement facility or some kind of governmental building.

They heard a woman call Dill, "sir."

Billy discovered a sign that said, "Parole office."

Billy asked, "what does parole mean?" Mikey shook his head saying he had idea.

"I wonder what that means," Mikey said. He pointed at a sign "House Arrest Department."

Billy asked a big fat black woman walking up the hallway. "What is house arrest?"

The woman laughed. She said, "House arrest is a custody program whereby a prisoner is monitored through an electronic device that tells us where a person is 24 hours. The prisoner is usually allowed to go home but they must stay home. Sort of like . . ."

Mikey interrupted, "like grounded."

"Yes," she smiled. "Sort of like being grounded, except

that you are never never never allowed to go anywhere."

"Never?"

"Not until the sentence has been completed."

"Oh," said the boys in unison.

"Thanks," said Mikey.

"Oh, Miss," asked Billy.

"Yes, son?"

"Are people on house arrest usually real bad people?"

"Yes, son, they usually did something bad."

"Oh," replied Billy.

Over at Jimmy's house, Jimmy's mom was on the phone.

"Hello, Crissy? This is Wendy's Mom. Is Wendy over there? No? Ok, if you see her, please have her call me as soon as possible. Thanks."

She was starting to get scared.

Over at Lenny's house, Wendy and Lenny are becoming friends.

Wendy said, "Why are you wearing that gizmo? What did you do? Something bad?"

"They say I did."

"That thing sort of scares me."

"It is a real pain."

"So what bad thing did you do?"

"It doesn't matter. I am innocent. Just a big misunderstanding. One person lying to another person. Lying about a person. Normal stuff. Happens everyday in every home in America."

"How do I know you are telling the truth?"

He laughed cynically. "You talk just like my family. No one believed me, not even my own family. No one backed me."

Wendy asked, "How do you get the money for big screen and expensive furniture?"

"Just say it was a present from my Mom."

Lenny broke down, crying,

"One thing I learned in prison is that material things don't mean diddley. What really matters is the little things in life, the birds, the sunrise, good friends, clean air, freedom. Things that don't take credit cards."

Outside, down the street, Wendy's mom was going door to door looking for Wendy. She was getting angry and scared.

Back at Lenny's home, Wendy pointed at the gizmo.

"Can I touch it?"

Lenny put his hand on hers.

Over at the Federal Building, the kids searched for more information about Dill and Lenny.

Mikey went up to talk with an old guy in a police uniform.

"Sir?"

"Yes, sonny."

"Are you a police officer?"

"Well, actually I am a retired Border Patrol officer. I am working part-time here as a security guard.

"Hey kids," yelled Mikey. "This guy can help us."

"What's up here?"

"Sir, we are here to find out about a stranger who moved into our neighborhood who is on house arrest."

"House Arrest?"

"Yes," said Billy. "He is wearing an electronic device and he is being monitored by the corrections department.

"Yes, sir, we have a problem."

"Well, I am sorry to hear about this. Follow me to my office."

He felt sorry for them. He took them up to an office and a computer. He punched in their info into the computer.

Over at Lenny's House, Lenny looked down at his hand on Wendy's hand. Wendy was getting scared. She pulled her hand from his.

Back at the federal building, the security guard looked at his computer screen.

The name DILL was staring at him.

"I am starting to get info on Dill and his cases."

"What kind of cases does this man handle?" asked Mikey.

"It says he is a House Arrest Officer with the Parole Department. That means he deals with people on parole."

"Parole?" asked the kids.

"Parole is when people get out of prison, they have a test time where they are on guard that they cannot get into trouble."

"Who is the stranger, called Lenny?"

The security guard said, "I can't get into Dill's cases. They are protected."

The kids looked sad.

"Isn't there any way around that?"

The security guard said, "Let me try one thing." He punched the keyboard a lot.

"Well, it looks like he is working on a case in your neighborhood."

The computer screen flashed the words CHILD MOLESTER and RAPE.

The kids turned frantic. They ran away in a mad way. The kids all jumped into the car.

"Lets get home NOW!" yelled Mikey.

Over at Lenny's house, Lenny spoke into the phone.

"Dill. You have to get me out of this neighborhood before anything bad happens."

Dill said, "I thought you said you were innocent."

Lenny replied, "Well prison can change a man."

Dill said, "I'm on my way."

~

Outside, the kids screeched up in the car. They saw Jimmy's mom and some neighbors all in a crowd.

"What's going on?"

"Wendy is missing."

"Wendy?"

"Yes, she has been missing for two hours."

Millie walked up. She said, "I think I know where she is."

"What do you mean?"

"I saw Wendy over by the stranger's house."

"The stranger?"

"Yes, that man with the strange gizmo on his arm."

Jimmy turned insane. "My little sister!"

He yelled at his mom and the kids, "STAY HERE."

As he ran off, his mom started hysterically screaming. Millie began to cry.

Outside Lenny's house, Jimmy ran up. He started kicking in Lenny's door.

Jimmy's mom asked the other kids, "What is going on?"

"He is a rapist," yelled one kid.

"A molester," said another.

Jimmy's mom screamed at the top of her lungs. She became completely hysterical.

Jimmy's mom ran to a phone.

"Honey."

"Yes, what's the matter?"

Over at Jimmy's Dad's work, Jimmy's dad was crying. All the guys at work grabbed him.

One of his co-workers grabbed some tire irons.

"Let's go NOW!" they angrily cheered.

Over at Lenny's house, Jimmy kicked in the door.

He confronted Lenny. He grabbed him.

"Where's my little sister?"

Jimmy punched Lenny in the stomach.

Lenny pushed back at Jimmy, slapping him with karate chops him to the ground.

Just as Lenny is about to really hurt Jimmy, Wendy screamed, "Lenny."

Wendy said, "Lenny, you have seen enough violence."

Jimmy yelled, "get back, Wendy."

Wendy told Jimmy, "nothing happened."

"What do you mean?"

"Nothing happened, Jimmy. Lenny is just a guy with lots of problems."

Outside the house, the crowd was turning into a mob.

A car screeched around the corner. It was Dill.

He could see the mob headed toward Lenny's house. Dill

quickly pulled up to the house.

Dill jumped out of the car, pulling out his pistol.

The mob was not scared by Dill or his gun.

"Out of our way."

"Stop," yelled Dill. He shot his gun into the air.

Jimmy's mom screamed, "How could you bring a child molester to their neighborhood?"

Dill said, "He is not a molester."

The crowd became silent.

"He once was a teacher," said Dill.

The crowd wanted to listen now.

"He had a girl student with a crush on him. She accused him of rape. It was a town in the south."

He looked around at the crowd.

"Where mob justice ruled and Lenny got 20 years for a crime he did not commit."

The mob started to rumble.

A woman yelled, "Our daughters aren't safe anymore."

Dill said, "Lenny is harmless. He also has an electronic monitor on his arm."

Over at Lenny's house, Wendy picked up Jimmy, helping him leave the house. Lenny held his stomach.

Outside, the neighborhood got noisy.

Jimmy's dad and his co-workers with tire irons drove up. They were screaming.

They rushed towards Lenny's house.

Jimmy tried to stop his dad.

Lenny came out the front door of the home.

The gizmo started to emit a screeching noise. It got louder and louder until it became an incredible high pitched screeching sound.

The mob stood still for a long time. They screeching hurt their ears. They stood still until suddenly the screeching noise stopped.

Dill yelled to the crowd, "you have nothing to fear from Lenny. The monitor is designed so that when it is activated it sends off a loud sound for one minute and then if the criminal doesn't get back to ground central within 60 seconds, the monitor will put out an electrical charge of 10,000 volts which will disable Lenny instantly."

Lenny looked at the mob. He said, "How sad it is to be a stranger. When I saw this neighborhood, I thought it would be different, a place where people could be friends and neighbors with trust and good will."

The people listened in silence.

Lenny said, "I am sad that it did not work out." The gizmo had a light and it was definitely flashing a bright light.

The mob did not care about Lenny's story. They yelled more and more and they got louder and louder. People began to push at each other. They looked at Dill and Lenny.

Jimmy yelled, "Please stop."

But they pushed him away.

The mob grabbed Lenny. They violently took him away.

Dill yelled, "Stop, Stop."

They pushed him down to the ground.

The gizmo started flashing and flashing.

Jimmy yelled, "No, No, No."

Suddenly the gizmo shot off a loud, buzzing, electrical charge.

Lenny was toast.

A woman shrieked as if she was the one getting the pain. But you could see the pain in Lenny's face as the voltage fried his brain.

Wendy screamed and cried.

The crowd went silent.

Lenny's body was limp in almost a ball on the ground.

Dill looked down at the body and then to the faces of the crowd.

"Go Home," he yelled. "You have done it. He is dead. So go home. Go home!"

Jimmy started yelling at Dill, "It is all your fault for bringing him here."

Dill looked at the faces of the mob.

Jimmy said, "This is a good neighborhood, a regular neighborhood. He probably would have been safer in prison or in the roughest drugged out neighborhood than here. This neighborhood cannot stand strangers."

Dill yelled, "Just go home."

The crowd disbursed.

Dill said, "It is no one's fault. Wrong place at the wrong time. This was a new program. The government was trying to save money. This is a cost effective program."

Jimmy looked at the dead face of Lenny. Then he punched Dill to the ground.

Dill went over to the dead body of Lenny. He took off the gizmo from Lenny's arm.

Jimmy and Wendy started walking towards home.

SIX MONTHS LATER

Jimmy's parents and Wendy dropped off Jimmy at the airport.

"It is hard to believe my son is going to college," said the Mom.

They kissed him goodbye.

Wendy said, "you seem older now." She gave him a big hug.

Inside the airport lobby, Jimmy grabbed his ticket from a machine.

"One hour," he told himself. He looked around the lobby and sat down next to a little kid.

He was having a real conversation with the little kid when suddenly a hysterical woman ran up and grabbed the kid.

It was the little kid's mother.

She yelled, "Please leave my child alone."

She was frightened of Jimmy. She spanked the little kid all the way telling him never to talk with strangers.

Jimmy shook his head.

Inside the airplane, Jimmy looked for his seat. There were empties everywhere.

He finally found it. He sat down. He looked around, pulling out a magazine.

A man and a girl sat down next to him. The man was wearing a suit. The girl was gorgeous, wearing a mini skirt.

Jimmy tried not to notice the strangers.

The girl tried to start up a conversation with Jimmy.

Jimmy said, "I am sorry, I am a little tired."

The girl turned silent.

"Okay, no problem," she said. "I understand."

Jimmy looked over to the sad girl and felt like a jerk.

"I am so sorry. I am not a rude person, really. I usually am outgoing and friendly."

The girl said, "I'm sorry, sometimes I make people mad because I talk too much."

Jimmy smiled.

As the plane started taking off, Jimmy looked out the window. He could see the bright colors of the beautiful sunset. The plane was going off into the light, causing Jimmy's eyes to go into overload.

As everything came back into focus, Jimmy looked over at the girl and noticed a gizmo on her arm.

About the Author

Robert J. McHatton is the author of "MY KIDS," "THE DIRTY DEED" and "BONUS TIME AND OTHER STORIES." He is an award-winning filmmaker from Oregon. His films include "UMATILLA" and "SHIP OF MIRACLES."

You can learn more about his adventures at www.rjmchatton.com